BLOOD ALCOHOL

Serial Investigations 3

Rhiannon D'Averc

Copyright © 2019 by Rhiannon D'Averc.

All rights reserved. No part of this publication may be reproduced, distributed, or transmitted in any form or by any means, including photocopying, recording, or other electronic or mechanical methods, without the prior written permission of the publisher / author, except in the case of brief quotations embodied in critical reviews and certain other non-commercial uses permitted by copyright law. For permission requests, write to the publisher at the address below.

Rhiannon D'Averc - www.rhiannondaverc.co.uk

First Edition November 2019

This is a work of fiction. Names, characters, businesses, places, events and incidents are either the products of the author's imagination or used in a fictitious manner. Any resemblance to actual persons, living or dead, or actual events is purely coincidental.

CONTENTS

Title Page
Become a VIP   1
One – Will   3
2 – Ram   8
Three - Will   14
4 – Ram   24
Five – Will   29
6 – Ram   34
Seven – Will   38
8 – Ram   46
Nine – Will   50
10 - Ram   56
Eleven - Will   61
12 - Ram   66
Thirteen – Will   71
14 – Ram   75
Fifteen – Will   80
16 – Ram   94
Seventeen – Will   100
18 – Ram   115

Nineteen – Will	121
20 – Ram	125
Twenty-One - Will	133
22 – Ram	141
Twenty-Three – Will	148
24 – Ram	152
Twenty-Five – Will	159
26 - Ram	163
Twenty-seven - Will	170
28 – Ram	174
Twenty-nine – Will	179
30 - Ram	185
Thirty-One - Will	191
32 – Ram	202
Coda	206
Read More	208
And last but not least…	210

Also by Rhiannon D'Averc –

Standalone:

Boy Under Water - Dennis Nilsen: The Story of a Serial Killer

Serial Investigations:

Bloodless

Blood Evidence

Blood Alcohol

BECOME A VIP

If you love Serial Investigations, why not become a VIP? You'll get special goodies as well as access to books before they are launched to the general public. And you get to be part of the launch team for each book, ensuring that the series gains a wider audience!

To sign up, head to rhiannondaverc.co.uk/vip and enter a few quick details.

Author's Note

This story includes details of horrific crimes. They include rape, sexual abuse, murder, and torture. If you are uncomfortable with any of these subjects, please take care. While the version presented here is fictional, the crimes are inspired by a number of real-life cases.

ONE – WILL

In the morning, we talked about the weather. We talked about the latest news, uneventful as it seemed. We talked about breakfast.

Because there was no way in hell we were going to talk about what happened last night.

In my head, I blamed it on the alcohol, the heady high of success, even the junk food. Because I know that there are no normal circumstances in which I would ever have dared to kiss Ram, out of the blue like that.

Considering the fact that he, too, said nothing in the morning, I figured it was best to never talk or think of it again. The lingering awkwardness, Ram snatching his hand away after it brushed against mine by accident while making our morning coffees, was painful enough. I didn't want to risk making it any worse.

I was pretty lucky, really. Not everyone would have just let it go. I had been worried, lying awake all night and staring at my ceiling, that Ram might ask me to move out or never speak to him again. Then there was the nightmare that he might somehow let it slip to my parents, that the Ambassador would know he had wasted his life adopting someone like me, that they would cut me off as well. A little awkwardness was a small price to pay in comparison.

Still, I couldn't help my eyes tracking him from the sofa as he moved around, making himself a second coffee, pouring in a shot of whiskey when he thought I wasn't watching. I had to put all of this out of my mind. I had to get us back to normal again. I'd spent years loving him, playing the best friend, hiding my true emotions. I could go back to that. Anything was better than this tension, this unbearable elephant in the room.

"It's Alex," Ram called out from the kitchen, holding up his phone as he walked over to me. The screen was flashing up with a call, and he answered it as soon as he was within good hearing range. Switching it on to speakerphone, he laid it on the coffee table, between us. I noticed how he still kept his distance, not crowding in beside me as he normally would, and my heart ached.

"Morning," he said. "I'm with Will."

"Morning, both," DI Alex Heath, our one and possibly only friend in the Metropolitan Police Force, replied. "I heard you put the Ray Riley case to bed, while you were in Kent."

Ram nodded, even though Alex couldn't see him. "He was buried out in a mound on the local nature reserve. We went to see his fiancée yesterday. Not the easiest news to break."

I thought of the way she had collapsed into wailing and shuddered. Ray's wife-to-be had come to us out of desperation, wanting answers for why her fiancé had disappeared into Kent even though the police were convinced he had done so under his own steam. When we took the case, it had seemed like the classic tale of a groom getting cold feet. It had turned out to be so much more.

Yesterday, watching her mourn the love of her life, I had thought of what it would be like to lose Ram. That was why I had to act like everything was normal, and hope that he would too. That we would never bring up the kiss again. I couldn't lose him.

"The details came back over my desk. The Chief is being asked whether we want jurisdiction or not, and he's turned the decision over to me. I, uh. It looks like I'm being given a bit of a trial run. See if I can handle a bit more responsibility."

"That's great news," I said, glad to focus on someone else's good fortune for a change. "You think there's a promotion in the works?"

Alex paused. "Maybe," he said at last, obviously unwilling to commit. "It doesn't necessarily mean something will happen immediately. I'm just going to be under a bit more scrutiny, I suppose."

"Not necessarily good for us," Ram said. "Better be sure to get permission next time you want us to look into something."

"Actually, that's why I'm calling. The case is... well, it's getting a bit more complicated by the minute. This doesn't seem to be as simple of a murder as it looked on the surface."

"What do you mean?" I shot Ram an alarmed glance.

"You didn't get a good look at Riley's body, did you?" Alex asked. He seemed to know the answer already, continuing on without waiting for a response. "There are things that have come to light during the post-mortem process. Once they got him cleaned up, it was more obvious. He had a number of lacerations and wounds, all of which appear to have been inflicted before he was killed. It looks like there was more went on than we suspected."

"What kind of wounds are we talking?" Ram frowned.

There was a pause on the other end of the line. "We're looking at possible torture."

Ram let out a low whistle. I kept silent, my heart sinking down into my stomach. We had hoped we would find our missing person alive. To know that he was not just dead, but killed horribly, made it so much worse.

"There's more," Alex continued. "DCI Fairlight passed on that you had unearthed a potential connection to Simon Shystone, a young man who went missing in Sevenoaks a while back. We're looking into that possibility with real seriousness. Riley was somehow forced to leave London and go down there, and since they haven't found any other burial sites in the reserve, the line of thinking goes that Shystone may also have been forced to go elsewhere before his death."

"Fairlight is handing the Shystone case over as well?" I asked.

"Not exactly. It hinges on whether we can establish a strong connection between the two, and whether the crimes originated here in London. Strictly speaking, the murder doesn't fall under our jurisdiction, but the probable abduction did. It will be a collaboration between the two forces, either way. I get the feeling that Fairlight wants more hands on deck, so bringing in a joint task force will help us both."

"And you want us to come in as civilian consultants again, given that we have prior knowledge of the Riley case." Ram ran a hand back through his hair before stuffing it back into his jeans pocket. In that movement, he looked tired and drained. Probably my fault. If I could take back last night, return him to his usual sarcastic and cheerful self, I would. Even if that would mean never knowing what his lips felt like, the slight roughness of his blond stubble, the sweet, smoky taste of whiskey.

Even if I would have sacrificed everything else in the world to feel that again.

"Yes," Alex said, and hesitated again. "This is the early stages, so not a word to anyone. But we're also starting to track a number of other recent disappearances. Young men who seemed to have everything going for them, who left behind a fiancée or girlfriend. Or a boyfriend, maybe. We don't have the parameters down yet. It might all be a coincidence – two men gone missing around the same time but with no real connection. Shystone might turn up in Dublin or Glasgow or the Cotswolds."

"But your instinct is that this is something bigger," I said, stating the obvious for all of us.

"My first instinct is that this could make or break my career," Alex replied. "No pressure, but I'd like you to come down to the station tomorrow and officially join our task force. We'd like to do this in an organised way."

"Right into the lion's den," Ram said, making a face. "Oh, goody."

"We'll come in," I said quickly, cutting over him. I didn't want Alex to get the wrong idea. After all, this was our case – we'd earned it. And I, for one, wanted to know more than anything what had really happened to Ray Riley.

And, if I was being honest, I needed a distraction. I needed to get the taste of Ram's lips out of my head.

2 – RAM

We start going through our files almost immediately. It's not like it's not all fresh in our minds – it's only a couple of days ago that we were watching them dig up Ray Riley's body – but the investigation has a new light cast on it now. Using what we know about Jude Hargreaves, the security guard who turned out to be a killer, might help us understand what he was doing with Riley that night. Not to mention why he was involved at all.

"What I don't get," I say. "Is this thing of Hargreaves committing suicide in his cell. Was there no check carried out by the police?"

"Fairlight said they weren't able to keep him under constant surveillance," Will shrugs. "Could be just one of those things. Not enough staff, too many ways to trick the system."

"Or it could be something else. Something more sinister."

"You think someone inside the station helped him? Brought him the razor, or looked the other way when they found it on his person?"

"It wouldn't be a crazy thought. I mean, police officers and guards are as human as the rest of us. Maybe someone didn't mind if a man who went around stabbing young, attractive girls to death was taken off the planet forever."

Will hesitates, looking down at the files in front of him. "I doubt we're ever going to find that out," he says. "Inquest or no inquest."

"You're right," I sigh. "We've got bigger fish to fry, anyway. The point I was getting at is that we're never going to find out who

Jude was working with – not from him, at least. Or whether it has anything to do with Isabelle's murder."

Will frowns and nods, mulling it over. "Maybe we already have the answer somewhere in our notes, and these files. We just have to keep looking."

I sit down next to him on the couch and feel myself freeze. We're sitting exactly where we sat last night. When *it* happened.

I grab a folder from the table and start shuffling through the papers, hoping that Will won't notice what I have – and that it won't make him want to run a mile again.

By the early afternoon, we manage to put everything into some semblance of order. We take our notes about a missing person and see how they apply differently now that we know he was murdered. Combining these with the police reports, some of which we had never seen until Alex emailed them over, gives us a better overview of the information that we already have.

There are just a couple of things we still need. One of those is more details about Simon Shystone; all we know so far is that he used to work at both the Highcastle Inn and a chain pub in Sevenoaks, something we learned while investigating the murder of Isabelle Rupert. He went missing a while before our investigation began, and there was some rumour that he had moved abroad, though the police had no proof to support that. Whether it was all a coincidence or something more, I am dying to find out.

Maybe dying isn't an appropriate word.

The other thing we need is the post-mortem report from the coroner working on Ray Riley's body. And for that, we can only wait.

My phone starts ringing just as we are starting to put all of the pages away in a neat order, at Will's insistence.

"Can't get enough of me, eh?" I say, answering the phone and switching on the speaker immediately. It is Alex's name on the caller ID.

"This is hardly a social call, Julius," Alex snaps.

I instantly shut up. I haven't heard him like this for a long while. Stressed, harried. No time for polite conversation (or whatever my conversation usually passes for). He isn't one to use my nickname, so hearing my real name from his mouth isn't unusual in itself; it's the way he says it. Something is wrong.

"We've just found Simon Shystone's body," he continues, his tone short and clipped. "Pending official identification from the family. He was buried in a shallow grave in a garden in Kensington. The homeowners have just come back from six months in Dubai, noticed something odd about their lawn, and dug it up. Hell of a coincidence that it's happening now, but I guess we can be happy they didn't extend their stay in the Middle East, or we'd still be looking."

"Shit," I mutter.

"I agree with that sentiment. Preliminary findings suggest that the cause of death is somewhat similar, at least from what we can see. I'm getting a copy of Riley's post-mortem sent to you – it was completed about an hour ago. You're going to want to see it. The main difference we can see at the moment is that it looks like Shystone died from a stab wound to the abdomen, but the rest is pretty similar."

Someone off in the distance calls out for Alex, and he shuts off the call abruptly, leaving us staring at my silent phone.

It is only a couple of seconds before an email notification arrives. He must have his people working hard on this, disseminating information as quickly as possible.

"Let's see it," Will says, reaching out for my phone as I open the attachment.

"Read it out to me, then," I say. Our hands brush as I pass it over, his fingers curling momentarily against mine as he takes the phone. A shiver runs through me. Did I imagine the spark of electricity that flowed through his skin into mine? I drop my hands into my lap, then cross my arms, restless and uneasy.

"Alright," Will frowns in concentration, scrolling across the document. "General details, name, date of birth. We already have all of that... Here we go. We have burn marks on the skin, likely caused by severe electrical shock, on the arms, legs, stomach, and chest areas. Genital burns, also."

I wince. "Severe enough shocks to cause burns must have been a risk to his life in the first place."

"Looks like his heart gave out," Will nods. "Official cause of death is recorded as cardiac arrest. Induced by intense pain and electrical shock, no doubt. He also has multiple other wounds. Contusions to the face, abdomen, arms, and legs. Knife wounds – not deep enough to kill or risk severe blood loss, so probably inflicted for the purpose of causing pain – to the arms, legs, groin, face, chest, and abdomen. Burns to the soles of the feet. Those are not electrical. The coroner suggests an open flame..."

I phase out, the long catalogue of injuries so awful that I almost want to cover my ears. More than that, I am distracted by Will, his attention solely on my phone. I watch his lips, full and soft, and now I *know* how soft. I take in his eyes scanning the text, their look so different to my own with his Korean genetics. So beautiful. And even though I've always known what he looks like – always seen the fine bone structure, the soft and lush hair, the deep brown of his eyes – why is it only now that I'm realising how beautiful he is?

"... removal of the left nipple with what looks to have been a sharp knife or scalpel, as well as the top of the left ear. Multiple scratch marks across the skin in all areas."

I realise I should give some kind of response, forcing myself back into being present. "Poor bastard," I say, shaking my head. "He suffered."

"He suffered for a long time," Will agrees. "Stomach was empty.

No unnatural substances detected in his bloodstream."

"Nothing to dull the pain," I say, sucking a breath through my teeth. "Fuck. That's a bad way to go."

"This just got a whole lot more complicated. A man goes out to Sevenoaks without telling anyone, leaving behind his loving fiancée. He stays in a B&B for a few days, speaks to the police and tells them that he's fine, and then gets helped out of the door by a killer. Someone else picks him up, presumably, and then he is tortured to death, killed, and buried in a shallow grave."

"And meanwhile, another man is subjected to the same thing but in reverse," I add, sighing. "This is a headache."

"Not as painful for you as it was for them," Will snorts.

I shoot him a look. Was that meant to be a dig? I guess he still isn't happy with me after last night.

Last night, which is completely out of bounds as far as topics go. The last thing I want to do is talk about how I made the traditional and classic rookie gay mistake: kissing your straight best friend. I mean, talk about a fucking cliché. I practically just starred in my own coming-of-age movie. Which is not at all funny for a twenty-seven-year-old.

And what really isn't funny, not in the slightest degree, is the fact that I can't stop thinking about it. That I think I might be starting to feel something for him, something I shouldn't. I still can't work out which one of us initiated the kiss, or which of us pulled away first, but the one thing I know for sure is how horrified he was by it all. He got up and practically ran into his room, getting away from me as fast as he could.

But Will is straight. He's always been straight. He was so uncomfortable when I took him to a gay bar that I have no doubt about that. So if anyone was in the wrong, it has to have been me.

I just hope we can carry on not mentioning it, and neither of us has to get hurt.

He starts getting up from the sofa, which has me shooting him yet another look – this time, one of surprise. "Where are you going?" I ask.

"I'm meeting someone tonight," he says. It's matter-of-fact, but there is a funny kind of underlying tone. It makes me think he is being super casual about something that is not casual at all.

"A date?" I ask.

"Not a date," he says sharply, turning and closing his bedroom door behind him with such abruptness that I actually flinch.

Great. Too soon. Maybe I should never ask him any kind of personal question ever again, just in case he gets spooked that I might try kissing him one more time. Believe me, I am not going to make the same mistake twice.

And the jealousy that bursts open inside of me at the thought of him dating someone is nothing, nothing at all. I grab my phone and start scrolling through Grndr, wondering if I can find someone tonight to take my mind off things. Make me feel normal again, get these thoughts out of my head. I'm probably just sex-deprived, in need of a release.

But after half an hour of only swiping right on men with Korean features, I have to admit that I might just have a problem.

THREE - WILL

I dressed with care, trying on at least six shirts before finally settling on something that felt at least vaguely fashionable and flattering. An oversized grey sweater that hid my frame, black skinny jeans a size too big, a black baseball cap over my hair, and black sunglasses. At least if Harry didn't turn up, I could hide my identity and sneak out in shame.

We had been texting back and forth ever since I knew we were coming home. I wanted to make good on our promise to meet up, sooner rather than later. If I hesitated, I would be giving myself a chance to run away from the whole situation and pretend I had no problems at all.

It wasn't like I wasn't fully aware I had problems.

Ram scoffed when I emerged from my room, ready to go. "Not a date, my arse," he said.

"It really isn't," I insisted, feeling irrationally cross. Not a good start.

I headed out of the door before he could argue with me any further. I didn't want to be drawn into a discussion with him about which girl I was meeting, and having to tell him it was a man I was going to see, and then having to explain why I was fraternising with his ex. And having to deny being gay again, when I knew that wasn't the truth.

Not that they ever really dated, of course. Harry was just another of Ram's love-'em-and-leave-'em victims. Just another reminder of the fact that there was no way Ram took our kiss seriously. No way it was anything more for him than a bit of fun. Loving him as deeply as I had for so long, even in secret, I couldn't bear the thought of it all being just fun to him.

I had to get those blue eyes out of my head and forget about feeling the roughness of his stubble across my chin ever again.

The journey through the Tube passed in a blur. I was too nervous to concentrate on anything. I nearly missed my stop twice.

But soon I found myself standing outside a certain bar in Soho – not the kind that we'd been to undercover, loud music and fairy lights; a quieter place, with booths where you could sit and drink with friends, your conversation obscured by the tasteful, low music.

If I had been worried that Harry wouldn't show up, I soon knew that I was wrong. I spotted him standing at the bar through a window, and hurried over to meet him. I was self-aware enough to know that if I hesitated outside and gave myself time to think, I would turn around and go home without so much as saying hello.

"Will," Harry said, his face opening up into a beam as soon as he saw me.

"Hi," I said, hesitating as I reached him. I wasn't sure what the right etiquette was here. Did I shake his hand? Hug him? Kiss on both cheeks like we were from the Continent? Follow my Korean roots and offer him a short bow?

Harry took care of my confusion with a pat on the arm and a sweeping gesture towards the bar. "Can I get you a drink?" he asked.

I nodded gratefully. "Just a diet lemonade, please."

"Are you sure? I mean…" Harry quirked an eyebrow at me. "From experience, it's easier to talk about uncomfortable things with a bit of Dutch courage."

I took his point. "I'll have vodka in it, then."

I left him at the bar to wait in one of the booths, at his insistence. I sat and watched him chatting comfortably with the barman, smiling widely as he paid and gathered our glasses. One thing I'd noticed about Harry the first time we met was that he had an extremely expressive face – you could practically read his mind by watching him. That was why it was heartening that he seemed so relaxed.

He sat down opposite me, sweeping both of our drinks into position on the table before lifting his again to clink against mine. "Cheers," he said.

I mumbled my own reply and took a sip. The sharp bite of the vodka against the bitterness of the lemon was a wake-up call. A strengthening one, in fact. He had been correct.

I looked up at Harry, his ginger hair catching light from the window, a September sun just starting to go down. He was handsome enough, in his way, a kind of everyday boy next door vibe. I wasn't attracted to him, but I could see that he had good looks. His blue eyes – not at all the same blue as Ram's, but deeper and darker - were fixed on me now, questioning, waiting.

I sighed. "Right," I said, awkwardly.

Harry smiled. "Stage fright?" he asked. "There's no right or wrong thing to say, here. We can talk about anything you like. If you don't feel comfortable yet, we can talk about the weather. It's up to your pace."

"I wish you wouldn't be like that," I blurted out.

"Like what?" Harry asked, frowning. He even moved back slightly in his seat, physically taken aback.

"Nice to me," I said. I pulled my baseball cap off and put it on the table to one side, and scratched the back of my head. "If you're nice to me, I'm never going to get there. I need you to push me."

"Alright then," Harry said. He leaned forward again so that he could pitch his voice lower – for no one's ears but mine. "So, tell me about the way you've been feeling."

"Confused," I said, then twisted my mouth. "No. That's a lie. I know how I feel. I just… don't want to accept it, or admit it."

"Can you admit it now?" Harry asked.

He still wasn't pushing me enough. In reality, I knew that he was doing things the best way. It wasn't helpful to force someone into coming out. But it still meant that I had to gather up as much of my courage as I could, and down half the glass of vodka lemonade in one go, before I could answer him.

"I'm gay."

We both waited a moment, the words settling into the air. The first time I had ever spoken them out loud.

If I was expecting some kind of instant cathartic release, I didn't get it. It wasn't like in the movies or on TV. But it did feel good. Or perhaps it would be better to say, it didn't feel bad – like I had probably thought it would.

Harry reached out across the table and touched my wrist. "Well done," he said. "That wasn't easy."

I rubbed my forehead, using that as an excuse to centre myself and stop the moisture gathering in my eyes. "It's the truth," I said. "I can feel that now."

"How long have you known?" Harry asked.

I sighed and shook my head. "I'm not sure. For a long time, I didn't really think about it. I wasn't… interested, when I was a teenager. Then there was university, and I was more focused on studying than anything else. Then I entered police training, and I met Ram – Julius - for the first time."

Harry raised an eyebrow and nodded significantly. "Was that the first time you had been seriously attracted to someone?"

I hesitated. Things were so unclear, even inside my own head. There were things I had denied for so long. Things I had chalked up to other sources, like the fact I'd never had siblings or real friends and didn't know what it was like to be this close to someone around my own age.

"I guess so," I said. "I don't know when it really started. One day I turned around and realised it had been there for a while."

Harry nodded again. "I'm guessing Julius doesn't know."

"He didn't," I said, groaning and sinking my head down onto one hand. "Although he may have guessed something last night."

"What happened last night?"

I gave Harry a miserable look, feeling so disgusted with myself that I wasn't even sure I could say it out loud.

"Did you say something to him?" Harry asked, leaning closer with a gleam in his eye as he read my expression. "Did you... You didn't? You kissed him?"

I groaned loudly again and buried my face into my folded arms on the table.

Harry laughed, then quickly apologised. "I don't mean to laugh at you. I'm just surprised. Tell me what happened."

"We were drinking," I said, raising my head to prevent my voice from being muffled. "Eating fast food. We just finished our case. Well, one of them, anyway. We were having a good night. Then the next thing I know, Julius is really close to my face, and I can't stop glancing down at his lips, and then..."

"Wait, he was already close to you? Are you sure you kissed him, and not the other way around...?"

I stared at Harry as if he was stupid. "Why would he do that? He thinks I'm straight."

Harry shrugged. "For one thing, I know a lot of men who have ended up kissing a straight guy just to see if it would work. And for another thing, I've met Julius Rakktersen. I'm pretty sure his ego is big enough that he probably thinks he *can* convert with a kiss."

I shook my head. Harry was wrong, but that wasn't the point.

"Well, he wouldn't need to. I've been in love with him for years." Even though I'd known it was the truth for a long time, saying it out loud only seemed to increase my misery. Unrequited love has a bad reputation for a reason.

Harry rubbed my wrist again. "I'm sympathetic, I really am," he said. "I only thought I'd fallen for Julius for a few days, before the wool came off my eyes, and that was painful enough. The way he lives... it can't be easy for you."

I thought of the way it felt every time he brought another man home – or stayed out all night – and shuddered involuntarily.

"So, what's keeping you in the closet?" Harry asked, leaning back and settling against the cushions on his side of the booth.

I looked out of the window, through frosted glass, barely making out dark shapes passing by on the street. The sun was getting low enough that it was shining almost directly into my eyes. "Any number of things, I suppose."

"Got any specifics, there?" Harry asked. I looked back at him sharply, but he was smiling. He wasn't mad at me. Just trying to help me through it.

"My parents, for one."

Harry took a gulp of his ale and crossed his arms on the table. "This one I have experience with. Are they pretty conservative?"

"My father was the British ambassador to South Korea," I told him. "So, yes, you could say that."

"Did he meet your mother there?"

"Of a fashion," I smirked, though it was bitter. I didn't like telling people my backstory. It usually made them feel sorry for me, which I never felt I deserved. I had been raised with everything I could have asked for, with the proverbial silver spoon, even though I was born in the wrong place at the wrong time. "My parents were trying to escape from North Korea, to join family in the South. They were caught. I was a baby, so somehow the smuggler managed to get away and keep me safe. My real parents were killed. Ambassador Wallace had no children, so he and his wife – well, my mother and father – adopted me."

Harry squinted his eyes at me as I relayed the details, brief as they were. He seemed to be thinking deeply before he next spoke. "You feel a lot of pressure to be the perfect child for them. They gave you your life, essentially, and you don't want to rock the boat."

It wasn't a question, but I nodded anyway.

"Do you think that they won't approve of your sexuality?"

"I... I don't think I've ever really thought about it," I admitted. "I just assumed they would be angry. I mean, you have to understand. They're very straight-laced. They were the ones who instilled the need for study in me, to keep my head down and get a good education. And to go into public service by joining the police force, well, I guess that was their influence as well."

"Maybe you can cross this bridge a lot later on, but I think it's worth really thinking about whether you want to tell them or not," Harry said. "If they do react well, it could strengthen your relationship. If you genuinely think they would react badly, then you can leave things as they are. But most people end up feeling like living a lie is a lot worse of an option that inviting potential conflict."

"What was it like for you?" I asked. I almost regretted it; it was a personal question. But then, here I was, spilling my personal thoughts.

Harry smiled, but there was not quite the usual warmth in it. "Things were rocky for a long while. My parents had a hard time coming to terms with it. My younger sister was on board from the word go, but it took a few years before family dinners weren't awkward. My dad exploded when I came out, said a lot of things he probably didn't mean. It took us time to get over that."

"How old were you?"

"Eighteen," Harry laughed self-deprecatingly. "What a time, right? I thought, I'm off to uni, I won't need their support anymore. If it all goes badly then I'll be fine. I didn't realise it would make me even more homesick. Anyway, I found a good support network of my own. I ended up joining the Student Union in my final year, and then I was asked to stay on as their LGBT Officer."

"Is that what you still do now?" I asked. I could see how good he was with people – with me. He had the understanding touch of someone who had a lot of practice at being a listener.

"I ended up moving on through a couple of different universities, but basically, yes," he explained. "I'm the person who students come to when they need help and advice. Not just with their sexuality or identity, but with things like career advice and help with difficult landlords, or fellow learners causing problems. I've seen and heard a lot. There's very little someone could say now that would shock me."

"I guess my problems probably sound like small fry," I said, sheepishly.

"Don't ever think that," Harry said, leaning forward again. He had such an engaging way about him. "It's not about comparing yourself to anyone else. You've been beating yourself up over this, anyone can see that."

I shrank back from his hand a little, avoiding his touch this time. I knew what he was talking about. The fact that my weight had plummeted was obvious to anyone with eyes. I didn't need him being able to feel my bones through my sleeve.

"I, um. I'd better go," I said, turning on my phone screen and pretending to check the time.

Harry groaned briefly and put his hand over his eyes before meeting mine again. "I'm sorry. That was a stupid thing to say. I'm not trying to push you into talking about things you aren't comfortable with."

"No, really," I said, shrugging it off with a smile that I did not feel in the least. "I've been out long enough. I should get back home before Julius wonders what I've been up to."

"Let him wonder," Harry tried to reason with me. "It might make him figure out what he's missing, hey? Come on, please. Have another drink with me. We can just relax, shoot the breeze. No more serious stuff. I promise."

I hesitated, on my feet but still in the confines of the booth, halfway between coming and going. "Why would you want to do that? I mean, just hang out with me?"

"Are you kidding?" Harry's eyes lit up with amusement. "We got on well last time, didn't we? You're an interesting guy, Will. Funny, too. You see things that I don't. I mean, being a private investigator – that's such a fascinating job."

I sank back down into my seat, half-reluctantly. My pride almost had me walking away, but the desperate need for attention and interaction won over. "I guess that's why you ended up going home with Julius in the first place, is it?"

Harry bit his lip and laughed again, shaking his head. "I didn't even know about that. He just told me he was Mattias Rakktersen's son and I was away."

I laughed, in spite of myself. Ram's father was a literal rock star, and it had him landing in the occasional paparazzi shot. "I suppose that's one thing I can be grateful for. There's a certain circle of people in which my parents would be well-known, but they definitely aren't famous. Not to anyone but political correspondents and other ambassadors."

"You must have had such a different upbringing than me," Harry shook his head. "Did you move around a lot?"

"For a while," I nodded. "I didn't come to England until I was six, but I was brought up speaking English and there wasn't much new I needed to learn. Not compared to other six-year-olds, you know. I just grew up pretty normally. My dad was away a lot, but we stayed here after that."

"But they were… I mean… well-off?"

"Oh, yeah," I laughed, though awkwardly. I had always felt a little uncomfortable at the level of wealth my family possessed. "I never wanted for anything. Best school, best university. They were always holding soirees and parties."

"And here's me in a little flat in Lincolnshire, dreaming of the day I could get out," Harry said, shaking his head in amusement. "Guess where I live now? A tiny little flat in London."

We both chuckled.

"I'll get us in another round," he said, starting to get up.

"No, let me get this one," I said, reaching for my wallet – which was full of guilty notes, each of them whispering to me that I should never have let him pay for the first drinks. Not at London prices. Not at my level of privilege.

We ended up having a third round before we finally went our own ways. Harry was not just kind, but funny, and he had plenty to talk about.

It was about time, I thought to myself as I left the bar and headed towards the Tube, that I developed a friendship that I didn't share with Ram.

The irony that I only knew Harry because they'd slept together wasn't lost on me.

4 – RAM

I keep eyeing Will suspiciously, trying to figure him out. Where did he go last night? And why is he so cagey every time I try to ask?

He is giving me nothing, and naturally, this only makes me want to know even more.

If we weren't looking into missing person reports and sifting for cases that might bear some resemblance to that of Ray Riley, I would be sorely tempted to investigate.

The room around us is quiet – too quiet for me to start up a personal conversation. It's a larger space than the station in Sevenoaks, set up with desks and computers ranged throughout the room. Alex found us a space in the corner, apparently where no one else wanted to sit, and a stack of files.

The gentle buzzing of low conversations, clacking on computer keyboards, and hum of printers is cut every now and then by the shrill cry of a desk phone. Alex has been pacing around, checking reports and consulting with various other members of the task force, and generally looking like a man losing his mind all day long.

Dark rings around his eyes, and his auburn hair not as neatly combed back as usual. He looks stressed. I have a feeling that my usual banter won't go down well today, so I keep my mouth shut. It's unusual for me to have such a moment of wisdom, so I've decided to stick to it.

"This one," Will says, holding up a file.

I scoot closer in my wheeled chair to look at it. "What's the link?"

"Man in his mid-twenties went missing two weeks before his wedding. The prevailing theory here is that he had cold feet. There were a couple of television appeals, but nothing ever came of it. That was a year ago."

I lift the colour photograph out of the file, looking at it more closely. "I think I remember."

"Gregory South?" A woman with thick-rimmed black glasses and dark brunette hair swept up into a bun leans over to us.

"Yeah. The bride did the appeals, isn't that right?" I say. "They thought he'd run off to Spain or something."

"We had a few tips that he was hiding out there, but nothing ever came of it," she says, pushing her glasses up her nose more firmly. "He doesn't completely fit the pattern, though."

"Young, attractive man, about to be settled in life, leaving behind his family without a word – what doesn't fit?"

"His name," Will says.

I look at him, and back just in time to catch her shooting him a small smile. "That's right. Simon Shystone and Ray Riley – both alliterative."

I consider this. "It's a bit much, isn't it?" I ask. "How would you go about finding victims that fit such a precise profile? The first part is fine enough, but you're looking at high-risk victims, the kind that will be missed. To add a name requirement to it as well?"

She shrugs. "We can only go by the clues that we have. Picking up and moving these men around is strange, too. Most killers like to stick to one area – especially if they are carrying out some complicated ritual of torture."

I narrow my eyes at her. "Wait a minute. You're a profiler or something, aren't you?"

She laughs and extends a hand to each of us in turn. "Diana

Hunter. Nice to meet you both. DI Heath said you're civilian consultants."

"Serial Investigations London," I say with a flourish. "We helped find Ray Riley's body, and link the two cases."

"And catch the Highgate Strangler," Diana says, her eyes laughing at me even if her mouth isn't. "Don't worry, I've heard of your accomplishments."

"We're just happy to help out," Will says. Goody-two-shoes.

"Speak for yourself," I say. "I'm here for the glory."

Diana smiles at Will again, her gaze lingering on him. "Do you have to put up with this all the time?"

"Sadly, yes," Will smiles.

I glance between them. I don't like the way they're smiling at each other. I can't put my finger on it, but I… I just don't like the way she looks at him.

"Anyway, we'd better get on with this research. Missing persons aren't going to sort themselves into piles," I say, spinning my chair back around and passing Will a new file.

By the time several hours has passed, we have a number of piles spaced out in front of us. Men who had a stable family. Men who had alliterative names (only one of those, unsurprisingly). Men within the right age bracket, and then finally, men in the right age bracket who also have a family. Next to these is a much bigger pile: men who don't fit any of these profiles at all.

There are still far too many in the piles that could fit the profile.

I sigh. "They can't all be victims. Most of them haven't been missing for more than a week."

"Most missing persons do eventually turn up, one way or another," Will agrees. "It might be too soon to assume anything for some of them."

"There are over a thousand open missing person cases in the

UK," Diana puts in helpfully. I am beginning to like her less and less with each passing hour.

"Are you eavesdropping on us?" I ask.

"You're talking openly. And this is a murder investigation, and you are on the task force. So, really, it's not eavesdropping at all. It's called working together." Diana straightens her back primly, resting her hands on her knees as she waits for an apology that is going to be a very long time coming. This only results in making her breasts strain against the thin fabric of her black and white striped jumper, a sight which has no effect on me. I just barely resist the urge to check whether it has done anything to Will.

"What's going on here?" Alex asks, intervening right on time.

"Missing persons checked and sorted," I say, giving a faux salute. "Unfortunately, it's not done us a lot of good. We're going to need to narrow down the profile a lot more to figure out if any of these are linked."

Alex scratches his chin, where a day's growth of stubble is already showing. "Thanks, that's good for now. We'll work on it some more. Listen, I've got an interview coming up around lunchtime which will probably help us out a lot. Will you come back later this afternoon? You're free to do as you please until then."

I think for a moment about what it would please me to do, and decide that Alex doesn't know what he's saying. No need to actually act on it.

We barely manage to nod our agreement before he's off again, barking orders at a group of men on the other side of the room.

"He's stressed," I mutter, shaking my head.

"He's doing fine," Diana snaps at me. "He's a good DI. He's going to be an even better DCI."

I look at her with one eyebrow raised, performing a new appraisal. Has she just shot up in my estimation, or was that too hot-tempered a response for a simple work relationship?

"Let's get some fresh air." Will nudges me from behind, and I get up, leaving the task force base with more questions than I entered with.

FIVE – WILL

"We've got an email," I said, scrolling through the information on my phone as we walked towards the exit.

"Stunning," Ram said.

I rolled my eyes. "I suppose your dripping sarcasm has nothing to do with that little confrontation we just had?"

"What confrontation?" Ram looked at me with narrowed eyes.

I sighed and shook my head. "Are you going to let me tell you the contents of this email without delivering a blistering attack of insouciance?"

Ram opened his mouth, presumably to tell me that he wasn't being insouciant, but then thought better of it and made an impatient gesture for me to continue.

"It's a potential new client."

"Something interesting?" Ram asked. His ears had practically pricked up.

"Well, you might not like that aspect of it. Before we decide, let me remind you that we will be paid for it."

Ram sighed, tossing a crumpled-up receipt he had found in his jacket pocket into the bin on the way out of the front doors. "Go on, then."

"Our customer is a forty-something-year-old man, name of Pete Webster. He is convinced his wife is cheating on him."

Ram groaned out loud, making a noise as if I had just punched him in the stomach. A few curious glances came our way, not least from the police officer just getting out of his car as we passed.

"Enough with the melodrama," I hushed him. "As I said, this is paid. We can't live forever on the money from the Strangler case."

Ram dragged his hands across his face as if his skin was melting. "Fiiiine," he conceded, none too happily.

"Alright. I'll email him back and let him know. He's invited us to come to his office around lunchtime."

"Wait, but what about our lunch?" Ram pouted.

I resisted the urge to tell him that we didn't need lunch. It would only lead to further confrontation. "We'll pick something up on the way, and eat it on the Tube," I said. "A sandwich, or something. Come on."

And I was true to my word. We did pick up sandwiches, and I did actually eat mine. I wasn't expecting it, but when we were standing in line I truly felt like I wanted food. I supposed I could justify it, with the work we'd been doing. It wasn't every day that we got to sit inside a real police station, helping out a real task force.

Truth be told, most of our work was more like this new customer – cheating spouses and missing jewellery that had so obviously been stolen by a nephew or daughter that it was worthy of daytime television. Getting the chance to tackle a case that actually meant something – that might help cut short this crime spree at just two deaths instead of allowing it to claim more – was special.

I soon regretted my over-large lunch, however, when we entered the accountancy office of Pete Webster.

"Sit down," he said, gesturing airily to two threadbare chairs in front of his desk. The worn surface of the desk itself was currently occupied by a large bowl of pasta – which, judging by the smell alone, incorporated tuna as well as the ham and sweetcorn I could see on top of it.

Combined with the rank burn of old sweat filling the room, it was enough to make me concentrate hard on not losing my lunch entirely.

"So, Mr Webster," Ram said, sitting down with only the barest moment of hesitation. If you weren't watching for it, you wouldn't have known that he found the scent of the room just as offensive as I did. "Tell us about your wife."

Webster grimaced, reaching out with a flabby hand to turn around a framed photograph on his desk. It showed him and his wife on their wedding day, obviously some years before. They both wore hairstyles and clothing that were last fashionable in the 1990s, and he was significantly slimmer.

"Ann's been cheating on me," he announced.

"Are you sure about that, Mr Webster?" Ram asked. "Do you have any proof?"

"No," Webster grunted, tucking his chin. A roll of fat threatened to absorb his jawline right into his neck. "That's what I want you two to figure out."

"You want her followed?" I asked, finding my tongue again. It was a struggle not to audibly gag, but I managed it, even when the expelled air of my words forced me to breathe deeper.

"I know when she's doing it. She stays at the office late, so she says. Don't believe a word of it. She's sleeping with some other bloke."

"And does this happen on a regular basis, or a random schedule?" Ram asked, his eyes roaming the room as he spoke. I followed his gaze and took in a diploma certificate and Employee of the Year Award, both dating back more than twenty years. There were yellowish stains at the top of the walls, likely nicotine. Between a few battered filing cabinets, our chairs, and the desk, there wasn't a lot of room for manoeuvre.

"It's random." Webster took a spoonful of the horrific mess that served for his lunch and paused with it halfway to his mouth.

"She'll call to say she'll be late. When she finally comes home, she's in a better mood than she's been in ten years. She gets this glow about her."

The fork disappeared into his gaping maw, his bulging cheeks chewing up and down as he ate with his mouth open. I had to look away. A limp houseplant in the corner of the room, its leaves mottled with black spots, served as a focal point.

"Have you confronted your wife about this?" Ram asked.

"Ann's smarter than that. I ask her what she's doing at the office late, she gives me this stuff about spreadsheets and deadlines and flexible working colleagues. She'll even tell me days in advance, like it's a planned meeting or a project running overtime. She thinks I was born yesterday. I know she's doing it."

"Alright," Ram said, with a decisive air. He leaned forward towards Webster, though how he managed to lean into that foul miasma I had no idea. "Here's what we'll do. You take my card, here, and give me a call whenever Ann tells you she's working late. We'll go to her workplace and watch the exit, wait for her to emerge, and follow her. If we catch her in the act, we'll bring you photographic evidence."

Webster nodded thoughtfully, wiping the back of his hand across his flapping lips. "And I only have to pay you for the times I call you out?"

I held in a sigh when Ram nodded. I wanted to be paid danger money for ever coming into close quarters with this man. I didn't feel like ever doing it again. "Plus a general investigation charge for our preliminary checks. We'll go into her social media accounts, emails if we can get to them. Start establishing potential partners."

"Alright," he said. "I'll give you a call."

"Mr Webster?" Ram added, as the man turned back to his lunch.

"Yes?"

"Payment in advance for at least four hours to cover each call-out, please. And the general investigation fee now, if you wouldn't mind."

6 – RAM

"I don't fucking blame her," I say, looking at the blown-up image of Ann Webster from one of her many social media profiles. "They might have been better matched when they got married, but now he's way out of his depth."

Ann was blonde, still slim and perky, with a smile that seemed to have only improved with age. Judging by the images of her with her friends, and the comments they left, it seemed she was the life of the party, too. Not someone who would want to be associated with a fat, slobby dick of a man like Pete.

Who, judging by his own social media pages, was at the very least Islamophobic, if not downright racist.

"Well, she could just get a divorce," Will points out. "She doesn't need to go on living with the man if she's fallen out of love with him."

"Two kids," I say. "Grown up now, but who knows? Maybe she feels a sense of loyalty."

"Then she shouldn't sleep around."

I remember how touchy Will got last time cheating came up, and decide to back off. I don't want him to think I actually condone this kind of behaviour, but maybe I don't see it in quite the same harsh light he does. God forbid anyone should ever cheat on him in the future. He has a lot of books about serial killers, and he knows how all the best ones got away with it.

Okay, that's not funny. I don't know what's wrong with me today. That kiss seems to have thrown my nose out of joint.

This whole thing would be a lot easier if I could just figure out what Will is thinking.

"There's one guy," Will says, spinning his screen around to show me. "Seems to comment on each of her posts here. Have you found him before?"

I squint at the username and shake my head. "Doesn't ring a bell. Bring up his profile?"

Aha – there's something. I tap a few buttons on my own laptop and bring it next to Will's, comparing our screens side by side.

"That's him," Will nods.

"Yeah, he's all over her statuses and photos here, too. Lots of compliments."

"You look into him. I'm going to see about her emails. Might be that she has one of those obvious passwords."

I continue my research, glancing up at Will from time to time. Just long enough to grab a picture of him that I can hold and examine in my mind afterwards, not long enough for him to notice. I don't want him to know that I'm watching him. Judging by his serious expression, maybe he wouldn't have seen it anyway.

I can't get that kiss out of my head. I don't know why. I mean, it's not like it was my first kiss. Or my hundred-and-first.

But I keep thinking about how soft his lips were against mine, and the scent of his hair, that expensive Korean shampoo he imports. How my heart leapt into my throat and my pulse quickened, and something thrilling slid through my veins.

I wanted to kiss him – like, really wanted to kiss him. Not just because I was looking for a quick fuck and I have an oral fixation. Like I would have just carried on kissing him, and nothing else, because it felt good enough by itself.

It felt so familiar, even though we've never kissed before. It felt, somehow, right. It was only for a moment, but I knew right away that I wanted that moment to come again.

And now I'm fucked, because Will is my best friend and business partner, and also happens to be straight. So fantasising about kissing him is absolutely not on my to-do list, now, or ever. I just have to suck it up and get over it.

This man on Anne Webster's friends list – all of her friends lists, actually. He seems to respond to every single thing she does, even if only with a 'like'. They talk about work, and a glance at his own profile tells me that they do indeed work together in an admin office for a larger corporation. Have both been working there for several years, in fact.

So, they may well be close. But then again, she also has a number of female friends from the same department who also interact with her frequently. And although I scroll down and down, trawling through months' worth of content, I can't find anything that would cross the line into flirtatious behaviour. There's also no hint that they spend time together outside of work, or that they have personal knowledge beyond what would be expected of colleagues.

I look up at Will again, my eyes caught by the sharp line of his cheekbones, trapping me down towards his mouth, held by his teeth at one side of his lower lip, a gesture of concentration. Fuck. No. Look away.

"I can't find anything incriminating," I say, deliberately keeping my eyes on my screen.

"I'm striking out with the passwords," Will says, sighing and stretching his arms up above his head. The bottom of his t-shirt lifts up only slightly, enough to show just a tiny hint of skin – and empty air, confirming the fact that his clothes are always oversized to make him look bigger. I've noticed it over time, his body shrinking while his wardrobe remains the same size, as if he thinks I won't be able to tell the difference.

And here we are again, remembering that I shouldn't be even *thinking* of anything resembling a romantic connection with Will – who, again, is straight - when he's already so fucked up that he can't take care of himself.

"Can you do some, you know, Hollywood-style hacking?" I ask.

Will laughs. "If you mean type really fast while lines of code go by on my screen until I get it, no. I could bruteforce it, but we could be here for years waiting for that to give us a result. Besides, we're working directly with the police right now, and I don't fancy going to prison for hacking on some two-bit cheating spouse case."

"You have a point," I say. "Well, I don't know that we found anything useful at all. I guess we'll just have to use our eyes and ears to figure out what she's up to."

"I hope it's a self-empowerment course, and she divorces him before we catch her," Will muses.

My turn to laugh. "As much as I think it would be cute if you were right, you might just be too optimistic on this one."

Will shrugs, brushing my comment off with only a faint flush in his cheeks, and closes his laptop with a smack. "We'd better get back to the station and see what Alex has for us."

SEVEN – WILL

"Come in," Alex said, gesturing into the room ahead of us. We filed in dutifully, faced with a television screen that was currently set to static.

We had been sitting around for a couple of hours, doing a few small research tasks as we waited for him to find us. He had said early afternoon, but it was almost time to clock off when he finally emerged. Then he had beckoned us over, stone-faced, saying nothing to anyone, and led us to this room.

Alex, Ram, and I arranged ourselves on chairs in front of the monitor, waiting expectantly. I had this sudden and almost hilarious image of us all as students waiting for the supply teacher to put on a movie. Of course, this wasn't going to be funny at all. Any video relating to the kidnap and death by torture of at least two men was going to have a distinct lack of humour about it.

Alex hesitated with the remote pointed forwards. "This... was not a fun ride," he said.

"We can handle it," Ram gestured impatiently.

"No, I'm serious," he said. "I've never dealt with anything like this before. Just steel yourselves."

His warning sent a shiver down my spine, even if Ram seemed indifferent. Alex wasn't exactly what you would call faint at heart. He had dealt with a lot of murders already, even in his short career. More than we had.

The screen flashed on, switching from static to an overhead view of a room set up for questioning, angled down to show faces and body language. It wasn't at all like what you would imagine from TV shows and films: there were bright, primary colours in the space, and comfortable-looking chairs and sofas. A woman, perhaps in her thirties, was settled in the middle of one of them. She was clutching a plush cushion in front of herself and already held a crumpled tissue in her hand.

"Katie, when you're ready," Alex said, his voice issuing from the speakers. He was not visible in the recording, but must have been sitting just out of view.

"I don't know where to start," she said, her voice hoarse and trembling.

"Wherever feels right. You can go through the whole account, and if necessary, we'll ask you questions along the way." There was a moment of hesitation. "Katie, I'll offer you again – you can speak with a female officer if that feels more comfortable to you."

"No," Katie said hastily, throwing up one of her hands towards him. "No, this is fine."

"Alright. In your own time, then."

Katie drew a breath, visibly shaking. She was thin, and the skin on her face seemed tight. Combined with the limp appearance of her hair and the deep-set hollows around her eyes, I put her down immediately as a habitual drug user.

"It was last year," she said, slowly, dragging trembling fingers across her face. "Can I smoke in here?"

"Sorry, Katie."

Katie sighed, hugging the cushion tighter. "I was working. On the streets."

"Were you a drug user at that time?" Alex asked, when she didn't go any further.

"Only weed," Katie said. "Sometimes a bit of coke. Just to keep me going, you know?"

She hesitated, scratched at the exposed skin of her lower arm, and then looked at the floor. "That doesn't mean I'm a liar. I'm not making it up. I know the difference between being high and something really happening."

"We're here to listen, Katie. We're on your side. I promise."

Katie breathed deeply, looking at Alex with some uncertainty. Whatever she saw there must have pushed her to keep going.

"I thought it was just a normal booking. A man and a woman – a couple. We get that sometimes. Kinky, you know? She wants to watch him with another girl, or he wants to watch her, or maybe they both want to join in."

"Where did they ask to meet?"

"They said they would meet me at a hotel. When I got there I rang them for the room number, but they said they were parked outside. They picked me up and I – I wasn't supposed to go with them. I was told not to change locations with a client. But they offered me extra cash, and said they wouldn't tell Robbie."

"Robbie would normally take a cut?"

"Yeah. He arranged the meetings and – well, you know how it works." Katie shrugged self-consciously, toying with the tissue in her hands. "It was a lot. More than I usually make in a day, just for a few hours with them. They said they just wanted to drive to their home, and they didn't want anyone to have the address so they wouldn't get harassed. They seemed safe. Normal. I figured that was a reasonable thing to say."

"Where did they drive you?"

"I didn't see. They made me get in the back seat, and the woman, she got in next to me. We drove away from the hotel and then she pushed something against my nose and mouth, and I blacked out."

"Do you believe you were drugged?"

"Yeah. Had to be."

Katie sniffled and looked down at her hands, remaining mute for a long time.

"Can you tell me what happened next, Katie?" Alex prompted. "What's the first thing you remember?"

Katie whimpered, her lips wobbling as she struggled to keep her voice under control. "I woke up strapped to this chair. Like a dentist's chair."

"How were you strapped down?"

"At my wrists and ankles, and at my waist and neck. No, it wasn't a dentist's chair. It was like – like a doctor. Like when you're pregnant."

A shudder went through me. I didn't like the way this was heading. Next to me, Ram subtly shifted closer, as if he was thinking the same thing.

"What could you see?"

"It was a small room. The walls and ceiling were bare, and they looked like concrete. There was a mirror on the ceiling, and I could see myself." Katie stopped and choked back a sob. "I was naked."

"You're doing great, Katie," Alex said. "What else?"

"There were tools on – on the walls. A couple of lights above me. Those were what reminded me of the dentist. And there was a staircase ahead. My... my arms and legs were held away from my body, so I couldn't cover myself up. I don't... people think that we wouldn't mind because we're sex workers. But it's not like that. I choose who gets to have my body. I choose who sees it. I can turn people down if I want." Her voice was running faster and faster, getting higher in pitch. Sobs were catching at the edges of her words, catching up with her, until she stopped and let them take over.

Alex's arm appeared out of the bottom of the frame, offering her a fresh tissue from a box.

"It's alright, Katie," he said. "Take your time. We're not here to judge you."

Katie blew her nose noisily and dabbed at her cheeks, taking a few long moments to compose herself again. "I was alone for a while," she said.

"What kind of tools were on the walls?" Alex asked, taking her back to the description of the room.

A shudder passed over her, easily visible even on the screen. "Knives. A saw, a drill. A hammer. There was this – box, this little box with wires coming out of it. It could shock you when they put the wires on your skin."

I noted her choice of words, distancing herself from the evil that had happened. *You*, not *me*, even though she was the one who had gone through it all.

"There was a whip," Katie continued on the recording. "Like, a… not like what you'd imagine. Short and stiff. I think they use them for horses or something. Not like… not like those long ones with the tail you see in films."

"That's good, Katie. And what happened next?"

"They came in." Katie stopped again and sniffled into the tissue. Tears were streaming down her cheeks, but she somehow managed to keep her voice in check. "Both of them, him and her. And they told me I… I had to do whatever they said. That they were going to hurt me either way, but more if I resisted. That they would kill me. If I did what they said, they would let me go once they got bored of me."

"What did they tell you to do?"

Katie closed her eyes. "Everything," she whispered, only barely detectable on the audio.

Alex hit pause on the recording, turning to us. He looked like he was about to be sick. "I'll spare you the rest of it," he said. "She went into a lot of detail. They held her for months."

"How long were you in there for?" Ram asked. His face actually looked pale, for once.

"Hours." Alex rubbed his forehead, squeezing his eyes shut. "I've only been out for fifteen minutes. I wanted you to see this as soon as possible."

"Why were they..." I stopped, wetting my lips. My throat was dry, and I couldn't think of a delicate way to word it. "What was their motive?"

"Sexual fulfilment," Alex said. His eyes were still closed. "She was little more than a sex toy to them. Both in the usual ways you would expect, and because they enjoyed inflicting pain on her. Katie told us the woman – they referred to themselves as Bonnie and Clyde – was the most vicious."

"How did she escape?" Ram asked.

Alex shook his head, finally opening his eyes again. "She didn't. They let her go. Dosed her up on a cocktail of drugs and turned her loose. Within days she was back on her old street corner."

We all stared at the screen for a few moments, digesting this information. They had been honest with her. She had cooperated, and they had let her go. That was something to hold onto, at least. If they had anyone now, there was a chance that they would still be alive.

"Why didn't she come forward to the police?" Ram asked, his voice cutting through our communal silence like a knife. He was frowning; he almost looked angry.

"She was high, a sex worker, a known drug user with an arrest history..." Alex sighed. "Much as I may not like it, I have to acknowledge that some people just don't like the police. She thought that no one would believe her, not after they did a blood test. No one had even reported her missing. She had sobered up in captivity, but the dosage they gave her when they released her sent her into a spiral. She's only just come out of a rehab program."

"Wait, how long ago was this?" I asked.

"A year and a half," Alex said, massaging his temples. His voice was slightly muffled as he leaned forward, placing his elbows on his knees and dropping his gaze to the floor. "And from the way she describes it, she wasn't the first. If they keep each victim for a few months, even assuming that they go through a period of rest between abductions, we're looking at far more than just Riley and Shystone."

"It's worse than that," I said. "This isn't just a serial case. It's a serial case with no pattern, no link between survivors."

From Alex's bleak stare, I knew that he had made the connection already. Ram was getting paler by the minute. "Not just men," Ram said. "Not just settled or happy with their relationships, not just leaving a loving partner behind. She completely throws off the profile we were looking at. What's her surname?"

"Wood," Alex said. "Katie Wood."

"No alliteration, either." Ram stood up with a jerk, his chair clattering over to the floor after him. "Fuck! All our research this morning was pointless. We're completely back at square one."

"Further back," Alex argued. "This morning we thought we had a profile. Now we have nothing."

"We have a survivor," I said. "That's something. We can learn from what she tells us. Are we absolutely sure that this is the same case?"

"She came forward after reading reports of Riley's injuries in the paper." Alex lifted his phone and swiped across the screen, logging into a portal and then handing it over to us. "Here. Hot off the press. They've just finished uploading photographs of her scars."

We swiped through the images wordlessly, taking in picture after picture of white, indented marks on Katie's skin. Burn marks, left by cigarettes and wires. A criss-cross pattern of lines on the back of her legs that must have come from the whip. Random, indiscriminate slashes that must have been cut by knives.

Enough to know for sure that the MO was exactly the same.

"Did any reports come back about Shystone's body?" Ram asked, handing the device back.

"As we suspected. Same catalogue of injuries. As far as we could see, anyway. He had been in the ground a lot longer than Riley."

"And his death?"

"Looks like he maybe tried to escape, and so they executed him. They clearly have a very specific pattern. The fact that we haven't heard about this before means that all of their victims are either dead, or were carefully controlled like Katie, until they were confident that she wouldn't tell."

Silence descended again. It was hard to know what to say at that point. We were probably all thinking the same things: how awful these crimes were, how terrible that they had managed to continue past even one instance. How difficult it was going to be now to track these people down – this self-styled Bonnie and Clyde.

And we were wondering exactly how many people were out there, harbouring silent wounds like Katie Wood – and how many were dead already.

8 – RAM

We sit in our flat, feet up on the coffee table, an old Western on the television. We're even both drinking a beer, something to take our minds off everything we heard today. Everything we didn't hear, which is filling our imagination with the worst things possible – and yet might, in reality, have been even worse than that.

And somehow, in spite of all of this, I can't fight my irritation at the fact that Will is constantly on his phone. He's texting someone, I just can't figure out who.

"Alright, who is it?" I say impatiently, as the credits roll.

"Who?" Will looks up at me with a startled expression that would rival a rabbit on the road.

I gesture towards his phone. "Your new girlfriend."

Will's expression changes; now he looks as though I've just announced I'm an alien from Mars and have landed here on Earth to teach the world the true meaning of lemon sorbet. "I don't have a girlfriend."

I roll my eyes. "Who are you talking to?" I could go with sarcasm, but it is beginning to feel as though the direct approach will be the only one to work.

"Oh." Will looks down at his phone as if seeing it for the first time. "Just... Harry."

I'm glad I'm not drinking at this moment, otherwise I would have sprayed beer across the room. "Harry as in... *Harry*? The Harry I slept with?"

"If you insist on identifying him that way, though I don't think it narrows it down very much. I would have gone with 'the Harry who helped us track down the Highgate Strangler', but fine."

I don't appreciate his snarky tone. "Why are you talking to Harry?"

"I'm allowed to talk to Harry. He's a nice guy."

"That doesn't exactly explain why."

"We're friends," Will says, throwing himself up from the sofa in a huff. "Is that so hard to believe?"

"I didn't even know you were still in touch," I mutter. My brain connects two things, and I swing my head around to watch him walking into the kitchen. "Hey, is that who you met up with last night?"

Will pauses in clearing away the mess I made when making our dinner, and sighs. "Yes. We went out for a drink."

I turn this new information over in my head. Harry and Will. Will and Harry. What kind of fresh hell is this? Is Harry trying to twist my best friend away from me, convince him to hate me too?

"You shouldn't hang out with him," I say, in a tone which I hope brooks no argument.

"Why not?" Will scoffs. "He is actually a genuinely nice person. Not that you paused for long enough to find out."

"That's why," I say, pointing at him. "That, right there. He's poisoning you against me. You know Harry hates me."

"I understand this may be difficult for you," Will says, walking back towards his room and pausing on the threshold. "But Harry doesn't hate you. In fact, Harry no longer cares about you at all. We just happen to get along, and it's nothing to do with you. Maybe try to consider the fact that someone might want to have a drink with me just because they like my personality."

With that, Will slams his door shut behind him, shutting me out.

I guess that told me.

Except it didn't, not really. He didn't tell me what I wanted to know. There has to be a reason why they are spending time together all of a sudden, and texting like schoolgirls. They weren't hanging out at all before we went down to Kent.

Were they?

I cast my mind back desperately, but I can't think of any unexplained absences, not to mention anything like this spate of texting. But Will is more… layered than I thought. First, I discover he is actually an erotic romance writer under the pen name of B.J. Wong, and now this. Secret bromances behind closed doors. What does it all mean?

It's not really true that Harry doesn't care about me at all, is it?

No, well, why wouldn't it be? Of course he shouldn't care about me. I certainly don't care about him, and that night we had together was a long time ago now. Nearly a year. Of course he should be over it.

But why are they suddenly so buddy-buddy if he doesn't care?

I have to admit that I sound peevish even inside my own head; it's not as if people wouldn't want to be friends with Will. He's right – there's a reason that I like spending so much time with him. It's not unreasonable that other people would see it as well.

I just don't like the thought of him hanging out with – with –

Well, if I'm being totally honest, with another gay man. Like he only gets to have one gay friend for his minorities quota, and I might be replaced. Edged out.

I get up and grab another beer from the fridge, then hesitate and take the rest of the box. I consider haunting the living room with the television turned up loud, but that seems petty. Plus, if he comes out to tell me to turn it down, Will is likely to try to confiscate some of my alcohol.

I retreat to my own room, closing the door with a deliberate gentleness. In here I have my own stash, the bottles that aren't for sharing with guests. This is a much more comfortable spot to drown out the self-doubt that Will's words have awoken within me.

I put on a rock radio station, wince and switch to a streaming service when one of my dad's old tracks comes on, and drink until the thought of being forgotten doesn't hurt as much anymore.

NINE – WILL

"This is impossible," Ram said, burying his head in his hands.

I turned a sideways glance his way. He would likely have been doing a lot better with this if he didn't have a hangover to rival a traumatic head injury. But I was too polite to bring that up. "It's going to be a lot harder than we thought," I conceded.

Diana wheeled her chair over to us. This time, she was wearing a plain blue dress, and her hair down around her shoulders. "How many have you got?"

"Hundreds," Ram said wearily.

The pile of missing person reports for men from London had evolved into both men and women from all neighbouring counties, to a depth of three or four in all directions. There were almost a thousand leads, and even taking out those who were already suspected dead or otherwise potentially identified, we were still left with the majority. There wasn't a whole lot more to go on – all we could do was eliminate those who looked likely to be a victim of something else, without anything to narrow the profile down.

"It's not a good start," Diana admitted. "What about narrowing it down to just those from London and Kent?"

"Already considered that," I said, wishing I could feel smug about it. Instead, I just had that heavy weight of defeat on my shoulders. "It still leaves us with over two hundred names."

Diana sighed. "I wish I could help more," she said. "This Katie Wood has thrown everything off completely. Until we can get some kind of clearer picture, either to their location or their reasons for choosing certain victims, I'm not having much luck with a profile."

A brainwave hit me. "What if it's because we're looking for two separate profiles?"

Ram and Diana both looked at me.

"Think about it," I continued. "We know there are two abductors in this case – Bonnie and Clyde. What if sometimes they grab someone to fit Bonnie's tastes, and sometimes to fit Clyde's?"

"I knew there was a reason DI Heath insisted you come in," Diana said, spinning hastily back to her desk and starting to type. Her fingers were a blur across the keyboard as she worked, watching the screen intently.

We rolled our chairs next to her, flanking her on either side, without having to discuss it. We wanted to know what she was typing.

It was a profile – a pair of profiles. A list of notes, taken down as a stream of consciousness, her thoughts flowing out onto the page.

Victim 1 – Male

Happily settled – family man

Missed by family

Alliterative names?

Wanting to disrupt happy family image, cause pain to family members?

Punishing a stable husband figure – link to past trauma?

Victim 2 – Female

Sex workers? Vulnerable

Not missed/reported?

Control and degradation of women seen as unclean or worthless?

There wasn't much to go on, even with that.

Diana was chewing on her fingernails, gnawing the rough edge of an index finger that contrasted starkly to her other neatly-made fingers. "It's something," she said. "We need to develop it further. It would be useful to find another female victim. I don't believe that they would have taken just one in all this time. Nor do I really believe that Katie Wood was their first."

"It was a little too practised," I agreed. "They had a routine down."

"It is still possible that she was the first," Ram argued. "With two perpetrators, especially if they are involved in a close relationship, there's room for practice. Roleplay. This could be a live-action extension of sexual play that they've been engaged in for years."

"It's hardly play. People are dying," I said.

Diana tossed her hair over her shoulder to look at me. "That's how it probably started. A fantasy. A game. These kinds of predators don't typically act on their impulses the first time they have them. It will have developed over time, from a mild, almost vanilla fantasy through to something more extreme, and then to real life."

"It's quite a normal process," Ram added. "You can see it in your own sexual behaviour. Or the porn you watch. When you were a horny teenager just discovering sex for the first time, vanilla was more than enough. Over time, we develop our own personal fetishes and tastes. They get stronger, more pronounced. It doesn't have to be illegal, of course. But think of all the people that get into BDSM and stuff like that. It's a short step from pleasure in pain to pleasure in pain without consent."

"That's the simplified version, but yes," Diana nodded, folding her arms and leaning back in her chair so that she could look at both of us. "Not everyone crosses the line. The vast majority of us don't. Most people don't even get into any kind of pain or humiliation play in the first place."

I was silent, mulling everything over in my head. Was I… some kind of freak? I hadn't ever spent that much time watching porn, and as for the smut I wrote, it was fairly vanilla in itself. I couldn't say exactly that I had progressed or developed any particular kind of fantasies. Not in the way they were describing. I had a sudden desperation to know if I was, well, normal.

Still, I didn't exactly want to speak up and ask Diana's opinion. No one wants to out themselves as the weird one.

"But what is it that causes that line to be crossed?" Ram asked. "How does someone go from play, from pretending, to something violent? Is there some kind of factor that goes into it, something we can track?"

Diana sighed. "The bad news is, not really. We can say what might be likely to cause progression. Often, it's a case of the lines being broken down in some other way – for example, if someone has themselves been a victim of abuse, they can be more likely to abuse someone else. But that doesn't go for everyone. We've seen abuse survivors who lead wholesome lives, never break the law, never harm another person – sometimes specifically *because* they know how it feels."

"And some abusers were never themselves abused. The cycle had to start somewhere," Ram added, darkly.

"Right. And there may be an emotional component which is missing in some cases but present in others."

"What does that mean, an emotional component?" I asked.

"For example, if a person shows psychopathic or sociopathic tendencies, they may not have that empathy for other people. In other words, they would not feel that they want to protect others from harm. Instead, they may even wish to harm others purposefully because harm was done to them. A kind of revenge on society, even though they may not think of it in those terms."

"This is all so vague," Ram huffed, raking his hair back from his forehead. "How are we supposed to find someone like this?"

Diana gave an apologetic smile. "Such is the nature of a profile, unfortunately," she said. "We can't really use it to exclude people or narrow the field down too much – especially as there's a risk that someone is simply setting their crimes up to give a certain impression, thanks to the proliferation of true crime shows and podcasts and books telling them what to do. But what we can do is use it to take an even closer look at suspects when we know they may fit the bill – and to try to figure out who may be vulnerable next."

"At least in that area, we have something, even if it is vague." I scratched the back of my head, thinking about the vast task that probably lay ahead of us. "But how are we supposed to protect every single sex worker and engaged or settled male in the whole of London – and now Kent as well?"

"You don't," Alex said, over my shoulder. "All we can do is warn people to be careful. And even then, I don't think it's a wise move at this moment in time."

We all looked at him for an explanation, swivelling around in our chairs.

"I'm keeping Katie Wood under wraps," he said, standing with his arms folded above us. "No leak to the press. She's information that the perpetrators don't know we have. They think we're just looking for male victims, so they may try to play it cautiously by only going after women. In the meantime, we can close the noose. Which is a lot preferable to them going underground, destroying all of the evidence, and running off to the south of France to start again."

"It would be France's problem if they did," Ram pointed out.

Alex scowled. "Thankfully I'm not heartless, so I consider it my problem if a murderer escapes on my watch to go and kill someone else – no matter where that might be. Diana, please don't let these two miscreants influence your way of thinking. I can't bear to deal with three of you."

All of us protested in some way – me with an objection to being tarred with Ram's brush, Ram with wide-eyed innocence, and Diana with a seeming dislike of being considered innocent in the first place. Alex just narrowed his eyes and stalked away, off to another group of officers, to repeat his warnings about keeping Katie quiet.

"Do you realise," Ram said slyly, looking sideways at Diana, "That your name means the same thing twice?"

"Hunter Hunter," she said, nodding primly. "I'm aware of the connection."

I could only laugh at the thwarted expression on Ram's face. Alex was right. He was a trouble-maker, through and through.

And me? I was beginning to realise just how boring I really was.

10 - RAM

"I think we should split up," I tell him decisively.

Will looks up at me with a startled, wide-eyed stare. "Why?" he asks.

It's true that we normally work together, and better that way. But we have two cases to work on, and we can't do both at once. Not like this. Not when one of them involves being present at a police station for most of the day.

And it's even more impossible, even if I don't want to admit it to myself, when being around Will right now is more of a distraction than anything else.

"Two cases," I say, short and clipped in my tone. "Two investigations, two of us. It makes sense."

Will pauses for a moment and even glances over at Diana's back. Checking that no one is listening. "I suppose you're expecting me to take on the Webster case?"

I smirk. It has crossed my mind, to leave him with the boring one. "No, we should share them both," I say. "When Webster calls and asks us to go into surveillance, we can't just drop a murder case. So we'll take it in turns."

"Fine," Will shrugs. "I guess it doesn't make sense for both of us to be exhausted from a long stakeout."

"Tell the truth. You're just excited to be working on a case that involves the use of the word stakeout."

Will chuckles but shakes his head. "I'm not excited about Webster at all. I just know we need to keep making money, building our business. We still haven't achieved a good living wage between the two of us, if you discount the payment from Coil."

J. M. Coil, whoever he was, helped us more than he realised. Will's right, as much as I hate that fact. We haven't been doing well enough to make a real living yet. Just another failure that I don't want to bring to my father's door. There's a reason I haven't visited them in so long.

"Anyway, this victim profiling stuff is too boring for me," I say. "You know I like getting stuck in. I want to go back over the murders, work it from that angle."

"Are you sure Alex is going to be okay with that?"

"Alex brought us on to consult, didn't he? He's better off accepting the help in the areas that we can provide it."

Will gives me a look, which I interpret as a rather-you-than-me. I am not going to be deterred.

I leave him at our borrowed desk with his piles of papers, and head over to where Alex sits in an open-door office. I knock lightly on the wall, getting his attention.

"Can I go over the reports on the bodies?" I ask.

"Which one?"

"Everything you've got. I want to tackle the victims while Will tries to look into who might be still missing. Is that alright?"

Alex quirks an eyebrow in my direction, barely looking up from his paperwork. "Since when do you ask for permission?"

"Just being polite," I say. I'm getting a sense of real tension from him. I'm beginning to gather that he is more stressed about this case than even I realised. I try to rein in the defensiveness in my tone and bite my tongue from reminding him that we're helping him out.

Alex gestures outside of his door. "Go see DS Fox for the reports. He should have a copy of everything you can look at."

I nod and back away, knowing that now is not the time – or the place – to confront him on his dismissiveness.

I take the files from Fox, who is evidently suspicious of working with outsiders from the askance way he looks at me and the slow way he hands them over. I retreat to another corner, an unoccupied chair next to a side table which nowhere near qualifies as a desk, and sit to leaf through the pages.

The images of the bodies are brutal. Like many things I've seen since I decided to join the police force back in 2013, they are things I almost wish I had not looked at. Only almost, because they will help me solve a case and bring someone to justice, and someone has to look at them. It might as well be me.

Ray Riley had been in the ground too long – his flesh had started to go. Not quite as badly as we saw with weeks and even months-old victims in the Highgate Strangler case, but enough that it still wants to turn my stomach. I clamp a hand over my mouth and an iron resolve over my insides, and keep looking. I can see the injuries described in the reports spread out in front of me – horrific injuries, the kind that would make me want to jump out of a window and end it all.

I've often thought about how I would do under torture. I mean, it's part of the job – looking at brutal killings, you wonder whether you would have survived. I have come to the conclusion that I would just curl up and die. The second they chopped off an appendage or knocked out all my teeth, or did some other kind of lasting harm, I would just give up. It would all be over. No point in trying to survive.

I've never been the type to be want to be applauded for my courage and strength in diversity. Fuck that. I would much rather face criticism for my easy life and upbringing, and how everything was handed to me on a plate. Why wouldn't I want that? It means I actually have a nice life, not daily pain and struggle.

I glance up at Will, at the far side of the room, chatting with Diana about something in one of the files. He would survive being tortured, much better than I would. He tortures himself every day. He's built up a resilience to it.

I guess that's why I can't tell if the thought of our kiss is torturing him the way it is torturing me. Because I can barely make it through an hour without thinking about it, and what it meant, and how I feel. And he hasn't shown a smidgeon of reaction since that night.

There he is, getting cosy with Diana. But didn't I want it this way? I'm the one who said we should work separately. I can't exactly go over there now and try to get between them. I shouldn't, besides that. So what if he wants to flirt with a pretty woman? He should. He deserves a bit of happiness.

I shake my head, a way to change my mental direction, and look back down at the page.

Simon Shystone didn't tell me much more. The same pattern of injuries – not specific enough that you could call it a ritual, but similar enough.

But then again, that makes me wonder. What is similar enough? The differences are just as big as the similarities. Some of the weapons of choice are missing – nothing torn off with pliers, no part of the body removed in any way. Only one burn point, and if my eyes aren't deceiving me, it looks different to Riley's.

What do I know, really? I'm no forensic expert. Maybe the difference just means that Shystone's skin is different, or the burn held for longer, or something like that. Of course, there is also the big difference in terms of the manner of his execution. All of this goes around in my head, and while I can't prove anything, I can't shake the feeling there is more to explore with Shystone.

Then there's Katie Wood. The bruises are long since gone, most of the marks disappeared from her skin. But there are scars and marks that match up. Burn patterns, slash marks. Things that you could easily see came from the same place, the same weapons. Much more similar to Ray's than Simon's.

I don't doubt her story for a moment. I don't see how anyone could.

But believing her means something much worse. It means that someone is out there abducting people, torturing them in all kinds of horrible ways, and then either killing them or setting them free – and we haven't even noticed for all this time.

And we don't know who they are, or where, or how to stop them.

It's going to be a long night.

ELEVEN - WILL

When the text came through at just past four in the afternoon, I was ready. More than ready. There was only so much time you could spend looking at the reports on missing people who still hadn't turned up before you would beg to be able to do something – anything – else.

It was my shift, my turn to follow Ann Webster first. So I packed everything up, grabbed my bag, and went back home. From there, I took the keys to the cramped, cheap little rental car we had booked for the week against the fee Pete Webster was paying and drove to Ann's workplace.

It was a nondescript office building, the kind that you walked by on every other street in London. Tall, but not remarkably so. Evenly-spaced windows on every floor, but not so wide you could see the whole office like you could in some of the more modern builds. When did we all decide that the ultimate luxury in architecture was to have everyone able to see everything you were doing at all times?

It was a bit of a shame, actually, because if she worked in one of those glass-fronted buildings I would have been able to watch her from outside. Instead, I just sat, parked across the road, watching the entrance and waiting for her to walk out of it.

I balanced a DSLR on my knee, trying to find a comfortable place to sit the heavy weight of the body and the unyielding length of the lens. It was all hard surfaces, switches and hinges digging into my flesh. I wasn't used to dealing with it – we didn't often need to gather photographic evidence, except in these kinds of cases. And even when we did, a camera phone was often enough.

It was only at a distance like this that a zoom lens was necessary.

I sighed, trying to find a more relaxed position in the driver's seat. I briefly considered getting out and sitting in the passenger seat instead, but that would have left me at a disadvantage: unable to get out and follow her quickly enough if she sped by in someone else's vehicle. I knew she was supposed to get the Tube home, but if she was cheating, who knew what kind of transport she would take.

The carefully scented air of the rental car, which still managed to smell somehow vaguely unpleasant, itched at me until I put my window down. It wasn't precisely fresh air – this was London, after all – but it would do.

Stakeouts were long and boring, and actually quite difficult. They were difficult because you had to stay focused for a very long period of time. You had to keep watching for something important, rather than allowing yourself to unspool into your thoughts and drift away.

You had to not think about things like your best friend's mouth, and what it felt like on yours only a few nights ago.

You had to keep things like that right out of your head.

I watched the clock and the door alternately until I realised that doing this only seemed to make the clock tick slower. Then I stared at just the door instead, challenging myself to see how long I could go without checking the time. I never made it more than five minutes.

I looked at the cars parked in the employee section, counting how many by make and model, then by colour, then even by number plate. How many of them were from the old letter system signifying their age, and how many used area codes. I watched idly as people walked down the street. Some of them saw me and reacted in their own myriad ways: startled to see someone watching, or crossing the road, or else barely reacting at all with only a flicker in their eyes when they saw through the glare of the windscreen.

And I considered how Ram had leaned in towards me and seemed like he was going to draw me in closer, and I wondered about what that meant, and whether he was just so far gone in whiskey that night that he would have reacted the same way to anyone.

And I just didn't want to think about it anymore.

I grabbed my phone and pushed headphones into my ears, one eye on the door and the other on scrolling through a podcast app. I found some true crime show to listen to, sinking back and absorbing the slow and deliberate delivery of the facts of a case I had never explored before.

This was my quiet place. My safe spot. With the podcast on, I could sink back into the cushions of the car seat and just thinking about some random killing that happened in Canada thirty years ago, and nothing else.

Studying had always been important to me. It is through studying the past that we learn how to solve, and even prevent, crimes in the future. This investigative tool or that psychological trick may the key to cracking a case we haven't even started yet. And the interesting thing is that history repeats itself. Though we like to think of ourselves as unique individuals, humanity is by and large doomed to commit the same sins as our forefathers.

Or mothers, obviously.

Thinking of parentage sent, as it always did, a rod down my spine. It forced me to sit straighter and raise my chin. Like the good little guest at the Ambassador's table, there to distract the political men with something sweet and adorable before they get to the real business. A showpiece to demonstrate how good a man my father was.

I shook my head at myself, scratching the back of my neck and trying to settle back down. That wasn't fair. None of it was. I wasn't a toy or a doll to be put on display. My parents rescued me and raised me as their own, with all the love they would have given to a real son. We had our own little idiosyncrasies and difficulties, as any family does. But they raised me with love.

I skipped back a minute in the podcast recording, taking a deep breath and trying to get my head back into the right place to listen again.

I sat there for hours. When her colleagues streamed out of the place at home time, only thirty minutes after my arrival, there was a flurry of activity which was difficult to keep track of. I strained my eyes, leaning forward, trying to figure out if any of the indiscriminately similar blonde heads bobbing out of the building belonged to Ann Webster. They didn't seem to. Not from the images I had seen, at least.

So, she was staying late. Whether to do some real work or to sneak off into a supply closet with a man she shouldn't, I had no way of knowing.

I sat and I waited, bouncing between some kind of semblance of calm as I listened to the podcast and that restless bout of thoughtfulness that came any time I was sitting on my own, doing nothing. No voices to distract me other than the ones playing inside my head, and since they were not speaking directly to me, it was easy enough to stop listening.

Eventually, I pulled up a messaging app instead, fidgeting in my seat against the long ache that was settling in my spine. I found Harry's number and fired off a courtesy, something bred into me by those childhood days when writing a thank you note was expected for any slight kindness.

- *Thank you for meeting with me the other day. It really helped.*

I didn't have long to wait before the reply came back, my phone buzzing in my hand and startling me.

- Any time. By which I mean, when do you want to meet again?

I smiled, reread the message, and smiled again. It felt good to be wanted. To have a friend. Someone who wasn't Ram – wasn't part of this strange, maybe toxic relationship that we had and all the baggage that came with it. Someone who didn't stand next to me in San Francisco, watching a man die.

At that thought, my stomach twisted and the smile soured. The reason I didn't have other friends was because I didn't deserve them. If I forgot that, I might as well jump out of a window.

Finally, Ann Webster emerged from the building. It had been so long that I had almost started to forget why I was there. I could have been there forever and not batted an eyelid. But there she was, emerging from the office in normal workwear, no sign of any ruffling or hasty re-making of her dress. No, she looked like a woman who was tired after a long day at work, and nothing more.

I almost wanted to slam my hand on the steering wheel in frustration, but it wouldn't have been much of an undercover stakeout if I'd accidentally set off the horn.

What a waste of time. All I had gained from this evening's work was uncomfortable introspection and an ache in the lower part of my spine from sitting still for so long. I turned on the ignition and drove home, knowing that this probably wasn't going to be the last day either Ram or I had to sit and watch a woman do nothing more than work late.

12 - RAM

I make a face. "Looks like it's my turn," I mutter out loud, looking over to the far side of the investigation room to lift my phone in acknowledgement. Will nods back, then returns to his perusal of a pile of papers which is noticeably smaller than it was yesterday.

It looks like he may be making some progress with narrowing the potential victim pool. Which is good, because the more information we can get about when and where people are being taken, the better. In the meantime, I am just beginning to feel like I am getting somewhere with my victims.

Both Katie and Ray were most likely taken in the evening. We know that from Katie's report and from the last time Ray was seen in London. With Simon it is a little more tenuous – there is a big gap in his timeline that has not been accounted for yet – but I think he may have been taken in darkness too. That makes sense from what we know about predatory behaviour. It's much more sensible to hide in the shadows than risk being caught in broad daylight.

I have also been putting together a list of the things that the torture room must require. We know that it is most likely underground because Katie says that Bonnie and Clyde always came downstairs to her. She also reported it being made of concrete, which supports the kind of home-made dungeon we've seen in the Josef Fritzl and Marc Dutroux cases.

Though I would like to take credit for that last connection, it was actually Will who sent me the Wikipedia page.

But I also know that the underground chamber in this case

requires a good electric supply, thanks to the use of lighting and the volts they zap through their victims' bodies. I know, too, that it must be either far removed from any neighbours or soundproofed. Since this is London, I'm going with soundproofed.

And then again, it could all be taking place in some remote location miles away, in which case that theory could dissolve rapidly.

Still, I think it's wise not to take any chances. If the police officers go from location to location thinking they would be able to hear any disturbances, they could miss something right under their feet. We can't afford for that to happen.

"Hey, Alex, I'm heading off," I say, poking my head in through his door.

Alex barely glances up. "Early, isn't it?"

"Another case." I put a few papers down on the desk in front of him, orientated for him to read. "I've been thinking about the bodies. Could be useful to analyse the dirt."

Alex stops what he is doing and looks up, albeit impatiently. "What dirt?"

"Shystone and Riley both had dirt under their fingernails and in places like the creases of their elbows. Could just be from where they were buried, could be something else. I've just been thinking about the way they were moved around from county to county. Would be interesting to know if they have any traces that can be tracked to a different location to where they were found."

There's a pause as Alex considers it, then nods briskly. "I don't see why not. It's a cross on a T, if nothing else. I'll get them analysed."

I nod my thanks, tap on the doorframe by way of farewell, and head back through the main room and out of the building.

Pete Webster hasn't left us much notice today, so I practically run to the Tube and through the streets home, grabbing the car keys from our apartment and heading out again as quickly as I can. To my relief, I get there just five minutes before the rest of Ann's colleagues leave the building. Seeing that she is not among them, I settle down with a bottle of Grouse and a sharing size bag of crisps for the evening.

I watch the quality of the light slowly begin to shift and change as the sun moves overhead. The late September days are still long, especially on those bright, sunny afternoons like this one. Even so, as the time ticks on, it gradually gets darker in this alleyway as the shadow of tall office buildings gathers around me.

I turn on the radio for company, but this only lasts a short while before the classic rock station plays one of my father's songs. I switch it off in disgust. I've never really enjoyed the radio, anyway. Opinionated, boring people trying to desperately find a way to fill five minutes between songs. If I want that kind of conversation I could go to any shitty bar and find the nearest lonesome drunk.

The Grouse keeps me company in the silence, but it steadily becomes far too loud. I wind down the window to hear a distant bird call – must be something nesting on top of the building – and the ubiquitous thrum of traffic and voices out on the main street nearby. The kind of thing some people might consider peaceful.

But there is a restlessness in me that demands more. I am more comfortable in the heavy noise of a club or bar, lithe bodies twisting around one another in a constant flow and ebb, lights and shadows, the chance of catching an eye. The excitement of the chase. I would far rather be getting a start on the evening's drinking in a pub than a battered old rental car that smells like upholstery cleaner and generic air fresheners.

I would far rather be doing anything at all than sitting alone, thinking yet again about Will and what happened when we got back from Kent.

I turn it around in my mind so many times that the edges are starting to get soft. Was it really the way I remember it? Did he linger a few seconds before pulling away? Was it surprise or just pure horror on his face?

It strikes me as odd that in all the years we've known one another, I've never really thought of Will that way. He has always just been a friend – out of bounds. I have known that he is straight from the moment we met. I made a show of myself the first day in training, deliberately. I like to separate the wheat from the chaff, so to speak. The people who can handle me from the ones who can't.

Though he had looked up at me and blinked owlishly behind the round, wire-framed glasses he wore back then, he had not turned away. Even Alex was dubious of me at the start. But somehow, even though I was the loudest one in the room and Will no more than a quiet shadow blending into the wallpaper, we were firm friends before the day was out.

I couldn't put my finger on it, but even at that moment, I felt like I knew. You wouldn't expect to meet and click with someone right away, create a lasting friendship by chance on your first day in a new place. But even then, in those first moments of conversation, I looked at him and I knew.

Except that if that kiss is anything to go by, maybe I didn't know at all.

I sigh, leaning my head back and checking my reflection in the rear-view mirror. I stare into my own eyes, tilting the glass towards me. I wonder what it says about me that my ego has been shaken so much by his apparent rejection that I can't get it out of my head.

I look tired. Strained, even. Thankfully, looking at pictures of dead bodies all day can do that to you, so I doubt anyone is going to pick up on it. I should hit the gym later, get some energy flowing. Work off a bit of the alcohol.

I start to play a game: every time I think about Will, I take a shot from the bottle. Refocus, sing a song in my head, keep watch on the office door. Wonder what Ann Webster is doing in there. Picture her either squirrelled away at a desk with her shoulders hunched over a keyboard, or pushing everything onto the floor to fuck her boss. Doesn't make much difference to me. I just wish she would show up so I could decide.

The sky is streaked with pink when she emerges, with nothing to tell me she was up to no good. A group of her colleagues, all looking tired yet elated at the fact of a project finished, a day of work done. A feeling I wish I could share.

Ultimately, this feels pointless. If she's up to something in there, we're not going to know. Not by sitting outside in a car. I should talk to Will, see if he can be persuaded to go snooping around inside the building. It might blow our cover, but it might also be the only chance we have to catch her in the act.

Talking to Will; that's another shot.

I'm halfway down the bottle before it occurs to me that I have to drive this car back home.

Fuck.

THIRTEEN – WILL

Saturday morning brought with it a light rain, drizzling down from a grey sky. I stood watching it from our living room window, admiring the slate and charcoal of the city, the occasional burst of emerald or rust down in the sculptures and bushes below us. A few kids with bikes sat on the stone plinths that were supposed to make our apartment complex look more impressive.

"Morning," Ram muttered, wandering into the room behind me.

I gave him a quick glance, enough to take in the bare chest and loose pyjama shorts, before turning back. "I didn't hear from you last night. I take it Mrs Webster wasn't up to any mischief."

"Late night at the office, by all accounts." Ram yawned and stretched, padding away towards the kitchen. "A group of them came out together. Unless they're getting up to something exotic, I'd say it was exactly what she said it was."

"Still doesn't mean she's innocent, though," I said. "We'll have to keep up surveillance for a few weeks to put Webster's mind at ease. At least. And that's if we don't find anything."

"Great," Ram said heavily, clattering about with the kettle and a mug.

I tried to refocus on the near-zen calm I had achieved while watching the rain, but the moment was gone.

"It's alright for us," I sighed. "For Webster, this is serious. He needs us to reassure him. He probably won't want the truth, if she is cheating. But he needs it."

"I don't see why it's so important."

I stared at Ram, then narrowed my eyes. This again? "You still don't think cheating is all that big of a deal, do you?"

Ram looked up, saw my expression, and only just held back from rolling his eyes. I could see the physical effort written across his face. "I just think that what he doesn't know can't hurt him. When he finds out she's been fucking someone else, what then? He's only going to get hurt."

"Ignorance is bliss, is that it?"

"More like chilling out a bit is freedom. I mean, they've been married decades, and they're only human. If she wants a bit extra on the side, does it really matter? So long as they still love each other – and I get the feeling that she could fleece him in a divorce if she wanted one."

I could feel a headache coming on at his words. "Of course it matters. They pledged themselves to one another. They got married. In front of their families, their friends, they said they would never sleep with another person again."

Ram shook his head, waving a spoon in the air as he poured boiling water into the mug. "This is why I don't want to be in a relationship. People are so uptight. Sex is just sex. It's different to love. You don't see me making a big deal out of it."

This is why I don't want to be in a relationship.

A shudder went down my spine. I couldn't prove it of course, and Ram wasn't meeting my eyes. But I could have sworn that those words were aimed at me.

Don't go getting any ideas about the other night, Will. It wasn't serious.

"Maybe that's why no one wants to be in a relationship with you," I bit out, harsher than I intended. "The only person you know how to love is yourself. If you asked any of the poor dupes you trick into your bed, you'd probably find they have a very different opinion of what it meant to them."

Ram blinked, then swayed a little on his feet. He looked like I had physically slapped him.

"I was just saying," he muttered, apparently his only line of defence.

"I've got some work to do," I said, swiping my laptop from the coffee table as I passed on the way to my room. "Don't interrupt me. I have a deadline."

And with that, I closed the door on his shell-shocked face, shutting him out completely.

It served him right. Did he really think that kind of behaviour was fine? He didn't seem concerned at all by the idea of cheating, as if it was just something natural that everyone would inevitably do sooner or later.

I fumed, pacing up and down my room, for longer than I would admit. I was letting him get to me, again. But those words of his stung, reminding me once again that my feelings for him were never going to be returned. No matter what kind of drunken pity kiss I could coax out of him, it meant nothing. Nothing to him, and everything to me.

I couldn't let him do that.

I hunkered down on my bed with my work, tapping furiously at my keyboard until I had something resembling a rough scene for the publishers. It wasn't very good, but I was angry. It was hard to write romance when you were angry.

Really, I was just killing time. We were due to head back to the investigation room for the afternoon, to join Alex in a little overtime. The team had just finished a seven-day stretch of working and were supposed to be taking a break, but Alex had informed us he was going to do at least a half day. Which probably meant he had been there since six this morning, and we were going to have to ply him with coffee and pastries to keep him going.

The intervening time gave me a chance to calm down a little.

If I was honest with myself, which I rarely liked to be, it wasn't just Ram's views on cheating that made me feel this way. I had known the way he was for a long time. It was the way he had dismissed me, just like that. No chance for us, ever, even if he knew the way I felt.

No reason to talk about the kiss, and what it meant, and why it happened.

I briefly considered the idea of killing off my main character in the next book. Maybe then I could stop writing for peanuts and concentrate on the business instead. Or, hell, maybe go home with my tail between my legs and start doing the kind of work the Ambassador had always wanted me to do. I had a history degree under my belt, I could use that for something.

And then I sighed to myself and pinched the skin on the back of my wrist absent-mindedly, feeling how there was still some give there despite all the weight I had lost. I was never going to leave. I couldn't walk away. To pretend I could was nothing short of arrogance.

I was as tied to Ram as if there had physically been string around the two of us, even if everything I felt was one-sided. He could use me as his dog for the rest of our lives, and I would put up with it happily, wagging my tail at every pat on the head and half-hearted treat he threw my way.

14 – RAM

I knock on Will's door, wincing to myself even as I do it. "Are you… ready?" I ask. I want to ask if he is alright, but I chicken out at the last minute.

There is a shuffling sound, coming closer to the door, before it opens and he frowns at me. "For what? We're not supposed to be going in until later."

"Alex called. He wants us in early. Seems there have been some developments with a test I asked for."

"You go in, then," Will says, irritated and already turning back to his laptop. "I'll join you later."

"He wants you as well." I have to interject quickly, into a closing gap between his door and the frame. "Something about an interview."

Will sighs and pinches the bridge of his nose, then turns with an ugly little noise in the back of his throat and grabs an oversized jumper. He pushes past me into the living room, snatches some shoes by the front door and slips them on, and leaves, while I rush to keep up.

Something I said this morning clearly rubbed him up the wrong way. But it's not like I'm hugely happy with him, either. *The only person you know how to love is yourself*. Kind of funny how the people you are closest to you always know how to cut you the deepest.

I put it out of my head, or at least try to, as we drive to meet Alex. We might as well; we have the car for a while, so we ought to put it to use. This way we can get across the city without needing to use the Tube or Will complaining about my motorbike.

"What have you got for us?" I ask, striding across the investigation room to where Alex has commandeered a string of desks to lay out large images and maps. I'm not in the mood for small talk, and I doubt anyone else here is either.

"You were right about the soil composition," Alex says, similarly skipping the ceremony. "The analysis came back."

"That was fast."

"I asked them to rush it. Doors tend to open when you have multiple homicides and potential missing persons linked to the same case."

Will and I circle around to stand beside him, looking down at the papers as he points things out for us.

"See here: these samples were taken from Ray Riley's body. The forensics specialists were able to differentiate two different types of clay in the samples. One of them is Weald clay, which you would expect in the area where he was found. This was on the surface layer of the samples. Underneath, in some areas such as his fingernails and pressed deeply against his skin, they found the second type: London clay."

"Am I right to assume that London clay wouldn't be common down in Kent?" Will asks.

"Precisely. More to the point, we know for a fact it isn't found in the nature reserve, because soil studies have been done there previously. London clay is a thick layer of the stratum – I believe that's what it's called – which is closest to the surface in North London."

We nod, musing over the maps and images spread across the table. "And this, here." I point to a map which has half of London shaded in red lines. "This is where London clay is most likely to be found?"

"Yes. We're having to presume that they aren't using heavy-duty digging equipment. If they were hiding the bodies at a building site, for example, there would be potential for it to be much lower. In some areas, this layer is down near the Tube, and at others, it is a more reasonable digging level. If we go with the theory that they would be digging with shovels, it narrows the potential area considerably. The thicker red lines, here."

"Well, that's a breakthrough," I say triumphantly, holding one of my hands up in the air. "We know that Riley was moved. It was probably just to try and confuse the investigation. This is still a London case, and Bonnie and Clyde almost certainly live here."

Alex leaves me hanging, glancing up at my hand and then ignoring it with a frown.

Awkward.

Will leans over and finishes my abandoned high-five, and shrugs. "Every little victory is a step forward," he says.

"We aren't stepping quickly enough," Alex sighs. "I can't help but feel this is a ticking clock. We don't know how regularly they snatch their victims. Either they already have someone that they are slowly torturing to death as we sit here looking at soil samples, or they're about to take someone. Goddamn it!"

With a growl of frustration that seems to rise from nowhere, Alex lashes out and thrusts all of the papers off the desk. They sail through the air in all directions, spinning and twisting like acrobats before dropping down to the floor, some of them folding in on themselves.

Alex pauses, seething, his hands clenched by his sides. Will and I exchange a glance over his head. We've never seen him like this before. In training, he was stiff and serious, and prone to not just sticking by the book but quoting it too. Since we made contact again, he has seemed confident and calm, in control. A man grown into his job.

Never driven so far to frustration that he would act this way.

The silence is broken as Alex covers his face with his hands, breathes deeply, and makes another small noise of frustration and anger. A more contained, restrained version this time.

"Sorry," he says, dropping his hands and gesturing to the hurricane still quietly settling around us. "I thought this was going to be a case that could make my career. Get it solved quick, get a promotion. It's turning into a nightmare."

Will drops to his knees and starts gathering up the scattered files, swiftly drawing them into a neat pile. I lay a hand on Alex's shoulder. "Don't worry. We've got this. You've got us on your side, right? And when you do solve this case, it's going to look even better on your CV than if it was some run-of-the-mill homicide."

"Right," Alex sighs, dragging tired hands over his face once more. "When we solve it."

Will finishes gathering the sheets and places them carefully on the table, aligned exactly in a precise pile and centred on the wood. "Which is going to happen very soon," he adds.

"I appreciate your optimism," Alex says, giving us both a lopsided and slightly sheepish smile. "I am starting to look forward to a good night's sleep more than the promotion, if I'm honest."

I bite my tongue. I don't want to mention that I don't feel like we are anywhere close to Bonnie and Clyde just yet. That, while I am confident we will catch them, I don't think we have a hope in hell of doing it anytime soon. Alex has a lot more sleepless nights in his future.

"What's next?" Will asks, glancing around the empty room.

"I've got an interviewee coming in," Alex says, chewing absently on his lip. "Another woman who claims to have been a victim. She's in with the team at the minute preparing, taking photographs and samples, and so on. I want you to come in with me to talk to her, Will."

Will gives a little start, like a drowsy kid in class hearing his name called. "Me?"

"I could do with another empathetic face," Alex says, looking darkly at me. "Julius won't do. But you have a good understanding of this case, and I know you're looking at the victim profiles with Diana."

"Why won't I do?" I protest.

"We're trying to help this woman, not intimidate her."

Will snorts, but then his facial expression changes as a series of thoughts flicker through his eyes. "Hang on – are you saying that I'm not… intimidating?"

Alex and I both chuckle, the sound alien and raw in this forbidding room full of crime scene photos and missing person files.

"Alright, Will baby," I say, clapping him on the arm. "This is where we part ways once again. I'm off for a drink to celebrate this win. You boys have fun, now."

As I'm heading for the door, I hear Will mutter something under his breath – something that sounds suspiciously like *of course you are*. I flick my head around to eye him over my shoulder, but he is studiously tidying the pile of papers once more, ensuring that they are exactly aligned at a precise angle to the table's corner.

Well, fuck it. I've earned a drink, haven't I? Even if there is still much more to do, every little success is something to celebrate. If you don't celebrate, you'll end up going mad under the sheer fucking weight of all the bad things that keep on coming every day in this job. If I never saw another picture of a dead body again it would still be too soon, but that comes with the territory. Can't have the glory without the guts.

I head off towards Soho and my favourite bar, trying to keep that little spring in my step at a hunch that paid off. Trying not to let the fact that Will is clearly still annoyed with me deaden any of the fun.

FIFTEEN – WILL

"He's still drinking to celebrate," Alex said, almost under his breath, like it was something he felt he was going to regret saying as soon as he finished saying it.

"Ram drinks for every reason," I sighed. "We're not going to solve his problems in one conversation, though. Not with something more pressing waiting for us."

Alex shook himself, nodding. "Right." He headed into his little office and plucked up a file, bringing it over to me. "This is all we know so far."

I run my eyes over the slim piece of paper inside, taking in the details. Jodie Reid, a woman in her thirties with several arrests on her record – mostly for possession of Class A drugs. There were details on her height, recognisable features, and a list of addresses, but not much else to go on.

"Is she ready for us?" I asked.

"Let's go find out," Alex suggested, gesturing towards the door.

We moved along the corridor and down towards a room set aside for victims who needed a more sensitive touch: the same one I had seen in the video recording of Alex's interview with Katie Wood.

I hesitated outside, looking down at my body. I realised only then that I was dressed so casually compared to Alex in his suit that I looked like I had walked in off the street. The black jumper, black skinny jeans, and casual trainers did not scream professional.

"Are you alright?" Alex asked, looking back at me with a sharp bite of concern in his voice.

I gestured helplessly, trying to find the words. "Is this going to be… alright?"

Alex paused, his hand on the door, holding it open. "You're a reassuring presence, Will," he said. "I do mean that. She will find it easier to open up with you there."

I blinked. Was he serious? Me, the skinny Korean guy with a temper that could fly off the handle into recklessness and a guilt that ate him away from the inside?

But he was serious, because he beckoned me in, leading me to sit down on a sofa and wait for Jodie to join us.

Jodie entered with another officer in plain clothes, a woman with a soft yet business-like outfit that spoke of comfort and professionalism. She seated herself alongside Jodie and nodded encouragingly. It was clear that she had no intention to speak, but was there to provide moral support.

"Jodie, my name is DI Alex Heath," he said. "This is William Wallace, my colleague. He is a civilian consultant working with us on this case."

"Like the Braveheart guy?" she said, darting a hesitantly amused glance in my direction.

I forced myself to smile and even chuckle as if I hadn't heard that so many times before. "Something like that," I said.

"Jodie, we're not here to judge you or to accuse you of anything," Alex said. His tone was gentle and strong, sending the message that he was steadfast enough to provide the comfort she needed. "I want you to know that we are simply here to listen to what happened to you and try to prevent it from happening again. We're on your side. If you feel too uncomfortable at any time, let us know."

Jodie nodded, sucking in a shaking breath. She was thin, with sallow cheeks that clung to the sides of her skull and sunken pits around her eyes. The cheap, faded cardigan she wore rose up a little at one elbow, revealing red marks that could have been scars just below the hem. A habitual user.

"How long has it been since you last used heroin?" I asked quietly, trying not to startle her.

She stiffened and looked at me with wide eyes, all the same, every muscle in her body going tense.

"We're not going to use it against you, or accuse you of lying just because you're a drug addict," I said, raising one hand in a gesture of surrender. "We just need as much information as possible to work up a potential profile for the kind of victim that might be at risk."

Alex was watching me subtly out of the corner of his eye. Perhaps wondering whether he had made a mistake. But Jodie seemed to relax, rolling her shoulders just a little to loosen them, looking down at the floor before meeting my eyes again.

"Last December," she said. "I'm going on nine months sober."

"Congratulations," I murmured, feeling a need to make up for the line of questioning. "Was that before, or after…?"

Jodie cleared her throat and squared her shoulders. Her face cleared, every line of emotion dropping from it. "They took me in May 2017," she said, like it was a simple and pure fact, nothing of any particular concern to her. She could have been reciting a history lesson about the inner workings of an economy that never crashed or boomed.

Alex nodded encouragingly. "Go on," he said. "Take your time and go at your own pace."

Jodie took another breath before continuing. "I was an addict. Had been for a few years. I was out of money and I was desperate. I ended up on the streets."

I watched her as she spoke, the way her lean, thin hands rubbed and pressed against one another. There was a half-moon shell standing out in relief on the back of her left hand, where she had pushed her nails into the flesh to get herself started. Her eyes were distant, fixed on some spot on the far wall between us rather than at anyone in particular.

"I was sleeping rough in Charing Cross station. It got…" she made a helpless gesture, glossing over whatever story lingered in her dismissal. "It was all men, down there. I left. Spent a few nights out in the open. I was begging during the day, trying to scrounge up enough change for a bit of food and a bit of gear. There was a dealer I would go to every night, if I had enough. If I didn't sometimes I would go anyway. Try and beg him."

Jodie drew in another shaking breath, a shadow passing over her eyes. She was looked back into the past, I understood. Seeing it as if it was happening right in front of her. It was real for her, at that moment – the person she had been and the things she had done. She looked haunted. She looked like she was trying to move past all of it, and yet here she was, getting dragged back there again.

"I was on the move, one night. I didn't have enough money for anything. He wasn't going to let me have any. I'd only eaten a sandwich that day but I just didn't have anything left. He shoved me away, told me to get away from him, that I was drawing too much attention. I went back to the road and walked, trying to think of something to do.

"This car pulled up next to me. A couple – a man and a woman. He was driving. They looked nice enough. A bit older. They offered me a lift."

"Can you remember the exact words they used?" Alex interrupted.

Jodie's eyes flashed towards him as if she had forgotten he was there. She swallowed, placing herself back in time again, nodding. "I think so. She said, 'Are you alright, love?'. I just nodded or something. They kept following me, the window wound down. She said, 'You look cold. Can we give you a lift somewhere? It's not safe out here.' I remember stopping and looking at them. I said I couldn't tell if it was safe to be in there, and he chuckled. Said I was a smart one. Then they... they looked at my arms and he said, 'Do you want us to give you a lift back to ours, to get some smack?'"

"They offered you drugs," I breathed. Less of a question than a statement. An idea forming. Some kind of grown-up version of the man offering kids sweets to get into his van. Katie was promised money – a lot of it. Jodie was promised heroin, the one thing she needed more than anything else. A temptation that was too much to resist.

"I said I'd go with them and I got in the back. It was a nice car. Smelled clean. Nothing on the seats or the floors. They just seemed... normal. Middle class, the kind of people whose kids were probably grown up and away at uni. It was weird. I started to think it was a mistake, they couldn't possibly have any drugs."

"Did they drive you to the house?" Alex asked, leaning forward subtly.

I knew what he was thinking. If she had seen the whole route, we had them. We knew where they would be.

"No," Jodie said, and the hope flooded out of both of us. "To a layby. I asked why we were stopping and he said he needed a piss. He got out of the car and she turned around to talk to me."

"Are you aware of where you were at that moment?" Alex asked.

"A residential area. I'm not sure," she said, shrugging apologetically. "I was already starting in on withdrawal. I didn't care where we were. I just wanted to get to where the gear was."

Alex motioned for her to continue, then laced his fingers together, concentrating on every word she said.

Jodie frowned, the next words coming out harder, straining from her memory like coffee through a filter, the more substantial lumps of information caught somewhere beyond. "She was saying something to me, something – I don't know. Something stupid. To distract me. He opened the door next to me and shoved his hand in, and everything got fuzzy around the edges."

"You blacked out?" I remembered Katie Wood describing the same thing.

"No," Jodie shook her head. "I was still awake. I just couldn't... I couldn't sit up, I fell until I was laying on my side. I remember staring right ahead at the seat. He was swearing at me, and she got out and sat down next to me. She lifted my legs onto her lap so we could fit. Then they drove – I don't know how long. It felt like years. I was just swimming along, trying to figure things out. Flashes of light on my face. Sounds – the car on the tarmac. It's all foggy, like it happened to someone else."

Alex nodded understandingly. "As a heavy drug user already, whatever they tried to knock you out with probably had less of an effect. Do you remember anything at all about approaching the house?"

"I couldn't move," Jodie said, her voice dropping until it was only just above a whisper. "He carried me. I was facing away – away from the house. I saw the car. Then she stepped in right behind him, and all I could see was her shoulder. I couldn't move my head to look up. I was swaying up and down with his footsteps. We were stopping and starting, rolling, going downwards, and then she was gone and I could see the stairs disappearing above me. Then I – then it went blank for a little while. I can't remember."

"You're doing really well, Jodie," Alex said. "Do you need anything? A coffee?"

Jodie shook her head. "I just want to get this finished."

"What's the next thing you remember?" I asked. I kept my voice low, soft, measured. I remembered the way the Ambassador used to modulate his tone when I was a child, soothing when I had scraped a knee or lost a favourite toy. How he still did it when I was a teenager, perhaps not realising that I no longer sought that kind of comfort from a parent. How it had made me feel better even then, even if I didn't admit it.

"I opened my eyes and the light was too bright." Jodie winced, closing her eyes, as if she was still there. "My head was pounding. At first, that was all. It felt like it was splitting open so bad I couldn't even feel anything else. Then there was the cold, the chill. It was a cold room. I felt goosebumps on my skin and that was when I realised I was naked.

"I opened my eyes to look and saw myself. Not just naked, but… tied. Held down in a chair. When my eyes had adjusted to the brightness a little more I looked up, and I could see a mirror beside the lights, see myself in it. I looked – god. I looked so… awful. I'd been on the streets, lost weight, the track marks in my arms. Unwashed hair. Dirty. I was dirty. I was…"

Jodie bit off the last words, drawing in a ragged breath that was more like a sob. I wanted to reach for her, to put a hand on hers, tell her it would be alright. But I knew that would not be appropriate. The last thing someone describing their own sexual abuse needed was unsolicited touching.

Alex moved a box of tissues closer to her across the table. "It's alright."

Jodie struggled to continue, opening her eyes and blinking, lashes flashing up and down quickly as she tried to contain the moisture that wanted to escape. She looked at the woman seated next to her, the silent watcher who had been a warm presence by her side all of this time.

"Will you hold my hand?" Jodie asked, her voice breaking a little.

The woman said nothing, but reached out and clasped Jodie's hand in both of hers, a grip that was soft and yielding yet warm and comforting. Jodie struggled in another breath, closing her eyes again as a tear escaped to trickle down her cheek, and gulped before continuing.

"There were tools on the walls. Like, DIY tools. Like I was in a shed or something. But we were under the house, I think, in concrete. The stairs were up ahead of me. I was so... I was so scared. I tried to look around more, but my neck was held in place by a strap. I couldn't see behind me or too far to either side. I thought I was alone for a long while, but then he – he spoke."

"He was in the room with you?" I leaned forward, eagerly. This was new. Katie Wood had described being alone when she awoke. That was more than a year before Jodie was taken. Any change in behaviour, any escalation, would be significant. It could denote even further escalation now, another year and change down the line.

"He was behind me," Jodie confirmed, gulping in air. Beside her, the woman winced slightly at Jodie's death grip on her hands. "He started speaking to me. He said I was his slave. Him and his wife's. He told me to call them Sir and Madam, but that their names were Bonnie and Clyde. That's how they referred to each another the whole time. H-he came around in front of me and st-started..."

Jodie trailed off, closing her eyes tightly, tears squeezing out of them all the same.

I opened my mouth, but Alex made an impatient movement, shutting me up. Apparently, now was not the time for enticements or reassurance.

"He started to touch me," Jodie rushed out, the words coming on the exhale of a breath she had been holding. "Rough. He was rough. His fingers were – they grated on my skin. Dry and rough. He told me I had to do whatever they told me to do. He started – he started – nnnn... He started putting his fingers inside me."

My heart clenched at her words, and the obvious struggle it was for her to say them. She looked to be in physical pain at the memory, the tears flowing freely now from her eyes, still squeezed almost violently shut. I didn't want to hear any more. I didn't want to know what had been done to her, what kind of people existed in the world that could do those things to her. I didn't want to have those images in my head.

And yet who was I? I had my own guilt, my own cross to bear. I wasn't a good person. I wasn't innocent and untouched by this world. I had things to atone for, and she needed someone to listen to her. I made my hand into a fist, clenching it tight under my folded arms until it felt like my thumb would pop out of the joint. And I listened.

"Cl-Clyde said that if I was good I would get a reward. And if I was bad they would hurt me. And they would hurt me anyway, but hurt me much worse. And the whole time his fingers were – were – and I tried to get away, tried to move, but the straps were too tight. And then she came down the stairs."

I wondered if Bonnie would have been angry that Clyde started without her. If she was an equal partner, or a subservient one. If their dynamic would change over time.

"She had – oh, god." Jodie stopped and gasped for breath, opening her eyes towards the ceiling. "Oh, god help me. She had a syringe. Spoon, lighter, the whole works. She set it down next to me and asked if I wanted it. I w- I wanted it so much. It was all I could think about. If I had that I could just stop thinking about the rest. She told me I could only have it if I satisfied Clyde. So I – so I – I did. I…"

Jodie broke down into sobs, covering her face with her hand, angling her body away from us. The shame that she still harboured was so apparent, etched into every line of her being. It was an impossible situation that she had been in. Nothing else for her to do but go along with what they wanted, or suffer more. Taking what thin pleasure she could find was no shame.

"You did what you had to, to stop the pain," I said.

Alex cast me a knowing look for just a second, as if smugly reminding me of our conversation on the other side of the door and my doubt that I would be a sympathetic figure. I could only find it in myself to feel a faint stir of resentment that he would even have the strength to give me that look. He had heard this before, from Katie; probably from other women, on other cases, who had been through things just as bad.

For me? It was just about the worst thing I had ever heard.

And so I had to blank my ears, still my mind, and try as hard as I could to only hang on to the most relevant details as she continued to tell us everything that had happened to her in that dungeon. How both Bonnie and Clyde had used and abused her equally, Clyde a man of sexual gratification and Bonnie more interested in the infliction of pain. How she could describe, beyond any modicum of doubt, that the violence and injury exacted on her body was enough to arouse both of them. I tried to take each piece of the puzzle and turn it into a profile, so that I could hang onto the profile itself and forget the details, forget the awful, keening pain in Jodie's voice as she described over and over again the sick fantasies they had enacted on her.

When she was finally done, I was drained, left a husk only, with far too many images that had seeped inside my mind despite my best efforts. I felt sick to my stomach, a twisting nausea that pushed back up my throat as I thought about the people who had done this. Bonnie and Clyde.

And I wasn't even the one who had experienced it all.

I had to wait until Jodie was taken out and we could leave, heading back to the still-empty investigation room, before I could let down my façade. My gentle smile combined with a pained expression which I hoped conveyed my sorrow for what had happened to her. Then, when it was just Alex and I left alone, I could finally sink down onto a chair and cover my face, overwhelmed by what I had heard.

"That was rough," Alex said, blowing out a breath as he sat down beside me. "Yet another victim who didn't feel she could come to the police. Four months of torture before they finally let her go. Even if we do manage to rescue someone at this stage, it's starting to feel like we'll still have lost."

I couldn't reply. I did not have the words, didn't have enough composure. If I opened my mouth to speak, I was sure that all that would come out would be a moan of horror.

After a long moment, I felt Alex's hand on my shoulder. "Are you alright?" he asked.

I took another minute, breathing deeply, sucking in air until I started to feel light-headed. "I, um," I managed. "I think I actually need to make a call."

Alex picked up on my strained tone and stepped away. "I'll give you a minute," he said. "I'll be in the office. Just knock if you want me."

I picked up my phone and called Ram's number. It began ringing, and I rubbed my eyes, waiting to hear his voice. One of the only things that made me feel like things would be alright. If I ever needed that reassurance, I needed it now.

The call rang, and rang, and rang. It started to dawn on me that it had been ringing for a while. And when the voicemail message kicked in, I only sighed and ended the call.

Great. He was out getting drunk again, just when I needed him. Would it hurt so much for him to look at his phone once in a while? Or even, god forbid, put it on vibrate when he was at a bar so he at least knew if it was ringing?

God, I needed him so badly. Not even in the way that I usually did – not that forbidden desire that had threatened on more than one occasion to ruin everything. I just needed him to tell me that everything would be fine. He was the one person in the world who could do that for me, and he wasn't even prepared to pick up the phone!

But then, maybe he wasn't the only one. Maybe there was someone else.

Now that I thought about it, maybe I did have another person that I could lean on, after all.

I called another number and waited precisely two and a half rings before it connected.

"Hey, Will!"

I smiled, closing my eyes, a bittersweet feeling. Here was relief. "Hey, Harry."

"How are you doing? I was just thinking about you."

"You were?"

"Yeah. I'm at a loose end tonight, I was heading out to meet a friend and they cancelled. I'm all dressed up with nowhere to go. Wondered if you'd like to go for a drink?"

I chuckled wetly, the noise getting stuck in the back of my throat behind all the other emotions that wanted to pile out with it. "That's funny. I could... I could really use a drink, actually."

"Is something wrong?" Harry asked, all warm concern.

I hesitated, the usual excuses on the tip of my tongue. The *no, I'm fine* and the *just forget about it*. That was what I would say to anyone else. But with Harry, I didn't need to pretend, did I? He knew me now – knew something about the deepest part of my identity, something that no one else did.

"Yes," I said, being perhaps more honest than I ever had. "It's work. I heard some things today that I... I wish I hadn't."

"Do you want to talk about it?"

"No," I said. "I don't think it would help. And I don't want to burden you with the same knowledge. Besides which, I'm fairly sure that would be illegal at this stage. It's an ongoing investigation."

"Do you want to sit in a bar, ogle men, and chat shit about nothing in particular?"

I smiled again, feeling it this time. "Absolutely yes."

I returned to Alex feeling a little renewed, a little stronger. He gave me a knowing kind of look, checking me over to assess my mental state, before gesturing to the desk where I had been sitting for the past few days.

"So, what do you think? We have a pattern?"

"We're starting to," I said. "I'd like to consult with Diana on this one, but I'm starting to see the difference between the two suspect pools. Whatever it is about the women they target, they don't feel the need to kill them. They are released, albeit harmed badly. What I'm wondering now is whether they target women from unstable backgrounds so that they won't be believed if they report it, or if they let the women with unstable backgrounds go for that reason."

"Whether it's cause or effect," Alex nodded.

"If it's cause, then it could be significant. Men from stable backgrounds killed, women from unstable backgrounds released? This kind of targeting could point to something in Bonnie and Clyde's backgrounds. Maybe parent figures, people who abused them in the past. It may even be playing out some kind of ultimate fantasy about themselves."

Alex shook his head, wiping a hand over his brow and down across his eyes. "Every time I think that humanity can't get any lower, the people of London manage to surprise me."

"Every time I think that there's no one decent left, they manage to surprise me on that, too," I murmured, offering him a slim but hopeful smile. "I'm going to meet a friend. You should go home. Spend some time with your wife."

Alex looked like he was about to protest, but then looked out at the empty room. "I suppose you're right," he sighed. "I'm not likely to solve this case all by myself."

"And you just did something that probably requires you to attend mandatory counselling sessions, so you deserve a night at home," I added, grabbing my things and heading for the door. "Don't let yourself feel guilty. This case isn't going to be solved overnight."

I turned away and headed out, catching a glimpse of him reaching for his jacket as the door swung shut behind me, satisfied that I had at least convinced him to take a break.

16 – RAM

I've almost finished my first bottle of whiskey of the night when I see them.

I'm having a good time. Getting drunk, blowing off some steam. Eyeing a pretty Chinese boy sitting at the other end of the bar, trying to work out if he realises what kind of establishment this is. Given that he has refused every offer of a drink so far, I'm wondering whether giving it a try myself would be wise.

And I glance away to the windows, and I see them.

The night has come down, the people passing by on the street illuminated by the light spilling from the windows. On this street, there are several bars one after the other, a place where people go after dark to find a good time. I like watching them pass, bodies that swell into view and then disappear into the distance, or else enter the door and my own sphere and become interesting in different ways.

I did not expect to see Will and Harry.

The sight of them together cuts me like a knife, swift and unexpected, a sharp thrust to my guts. My best friend and my old fling. And I still can't see or imagine or make sense of any possible reason that they could have for being together, except that Harry has some kind of plan to take me down.

He can't do that. Can't take Will from me. Not my Will.

But he's *not* my Will.

I close my eyes and I can still taste his lips, that soft sweetness. Something that felt like it had been waiting just for me. A ripe and ready peach, just waiting for me to come by and take it, untasted by any other. Mine.

Fuck, no. I can't fucking feel like this. I can't. Will is my best friend – the only person I have ever truly been able to count on. The only friend who wasn't just trying to get close to the money, or a big fan of my dad's band, or who used to have a poster of my mum on their bedroom wall when they were a teenager. The one person who has been there with me through absolute fucking thick and thin – through the worst days of my life and some of the best. I can't fuck that up.

I can't and I won't.

I need Will – need him just the way he is. My partner. My right hand. The person I can rely on when the chips are down. Complicating it with these other things – it won't help either of us. Will doesn't feel that way about me, and he never will. He's not wired that way. The look of disgust on his face when he leapt away from me after that kiss proves it.

These feelings that I've been having, the way his mouth won't get out of my head, it's all my problem. Not his. And I need to get over it pretty fast if I'm going to stop Harry from taking him away from me.

I dig my phone out of my pocket, dismayed to see a missed call from Will. Hours ago. I should have put it on vibrate like he's always telling me to. I'm just a little old-fashioned in thinking that it's rude to have your phone ringing or sitting in your hand when you're trying to chat someone up.

I swipe the notification away, thinking. Will won't be expecting me home tonight. And if I try to reach out to him right now, I might say too much. Might reveal too much of how I'm feeling, and scare him away even more. That's the opposite of what I want.

Instead, I find Harry's number. I search through my old text messages and find some from him, from the morning after that night we spent together. Pleasantries about what a great time he had, signed off with his name.

My fingers and thumbs flash over the touchscreen, firing off a message and sending it without giving myself enough time for second thoughts.

What are you playing at with Will?

I don't have to wait long for the response. They have long since passed out of sight of the windows, no doubt on their way to some other place, but I can picture Harry in my head slipping his phone out of his pocket. Reading the message, tilting his head, getting angry at the mere sight of my name. I know he still hates me, no matter what Will says.

Excuse me? Who is this?

I snort out a laugh, earning a look from the patron on the stool next to me. *You know who this is. It's Julius. Stop playing games.*

I'm not playing games. The reply is almost instant now, as if he is waiting for my response. *I like Will. He's a good person. We're friends.*

Stop trying to use him to get back at me

There is a longer pause before Harry finally replies. *Stop being so self-centred. If you can't actually fucking believe that someone would want to be friends with Will, that might just be your problem, not mine. Don't contact me again.*

I scoff at his warning, rolling my eyes. Doesn't hate me, my arse. I fucking told Will there was an agenda here.

Wait, maybe I shouldn't have messaged him while they were together. Will might get curious as to who he's talking to and ask him. Harry might tell him.

What if he shows the messages to Will?

Fuck. *Fuck.* Fuuuuuuck.

This is all stupid, anyway. It's not my business who Will spends his time with, so long as they're not crackheads and gang members. If he's not getting into trouble, it's good for him to spend more time out of the house. He might even consume some calories by accident. It's a *good* thing.

Will isn't mine. He's not, and he never will be. He is his own person. I just got too used to him being around all of the time while he was struggling with all of that stuff from the US. Maybe this is him getting over it now, getting back into the world again. Good for him.

I'm just too far down a bottle of whiskey to have sensible thoughts right now, that's all. Will's allowed to have friends.

It's just... I still can't shake this feeling that there's some kind of secret between them. Some conspiracy. And if it isn't about me, then what the hell could it possibly be about? Maybe I should send another message, ask Harry not to tell Will. Apologise, if I have to.

No, this is all stupid. I'm just getting myself tied up in knots inside my own head. Time to stop talking myself into paranoia and do something that will actually make myself feel better.

I slide over to the other end of the bar, and gesture at the bartender to give me a refill. Then I lean close to the pretty young Chinese man that I have been eyeing all night, turning on the charm to the fullest extent I know how.

"So, why are you sitting on your own over here, anyway?" I ask, as if picking up midway through a conversation we've been having all night. "It doesn't seem right."

He turns flat, disinterested eyes on me, affording me only the barest of cursory glances before looking away again. "I'm sitting on my own because no one in this bar is worthy of my attention."

Ouch. So it's like that with this one.

"Maybe you should look again," I suggest. "None of those other idiots bothered trying after you brushed them off, did they? Seems like you're just waiting for someone prepared to put up a fight."

He sighs dramatically, rolling his eyes as he deigns to meet my gaze again. "No, darling, I just have much higher standards," he says. "I'm not into drunks. I don't fancy cleaning your vomit off my shoes at three in the morning when you can't get it up and fall asleep on the sofa."

"I... I don't..." I flounder, trying to scoff and brush off his remarks. "I can still get it up."

"Go tell it on the mountain," he says, turning his shoulder on me so as to shut me out completely. "Or at least to someone who cares."

I retreat to a booth with my fresh glass, conceding that tonight might not be my night after all.

Outside the windows, I see someone else standing, looking in. A pale face lit by the warm glow of the interior, falling on a tweed jacket and a green tie around his neck. I stare back, recognition flaring in my mind.

The man turns and walks away, and he is gone before I can work through my memory to figure out who he is.

And then it hits me.

J. M. Coil – our mysterious benefactor, the man who paid us an obscene amount of reward money for catching the Highgate Strangler. It's funny: for a man who made a point of the fact that the gay community was his community, his domain, I've never seen him since. Not in a bar, not at a club, not on an app.

I get out of my chair and rocket towards the door, bursting outside to look down the street for him. I spin in a circle, searching in all directions. No tweed coat, not anywhere around me. He's gone.

Did I really just see that, or have I had so much to drink already that I'm starting to imagine things that aren't there?

I head back inside slowly, taking my seat and nursing my glass again, wondering what really just happened. J. M. Coil, here? Watching me?

I shake my head to myself and ignore the strange looks that other patrons of the bar are giving me. I'm under a lot of stress, especially with this thing from Will. Probably best not to be too hard on myself – and a bit of whiskey will make it all go away.

SEVENTEEN – WILL

Harry wasn't going to be ready for an hour, getting in some brief work on a Saturday afternoon to keep up with his caseload. Not unlike us, coming in at all hours of the week to get the case solved. At least, with it being the weekend, we weren't going to get any alerts to go and stalk poor Ann Webster.

I sat down with a notebook and some of the ideas Diana and I had been working on, in a little café a short distance from Leicester Square Tube station, where we had decided to meet. There was time to think about this.

What kind of things in someone's background would drive them to target stable men in committed relationships? What kind of things would make them target down and out women?

The women were possible outliers. Perhaps they were chosen because they were easy to take, often not missed, and hard to believe. But the men – there was more of a risk there. Case in point was the fact that it was Ray Riley's disappearance that had alerted us to any of this. So, if Bonnie and Clyde were willing to take that risk, it must have been for a special reason.

I started to form a picture of a broken home. A mother and father divorced, or maybe never together in the first place. A child conceived by – a single mother? A sex worker knocked up by a John? A drug addict who gave her body away for another high?

Whatever the case was, the father would have been absent. Not in the child's life. Easy enough to gain a sense of resentment about that.

I pushed it further: what if the father went and married someone else, became a family man with a stable life in suburbia? The kind of white fence family that his child couldn't even dream of?

I stared at my notes. I couldn't help but feel as though I had made some kind of breakthrough. It would make sense to target and take down men who looked innocent, if they were secretly screwing around on the side. Men who presented the same image as Clyde's – or maybe Bonnie's – father.

What was problematic was that we only had victim statements from women. We had no idea what had happened to Shystone and Riley, and why – whether they were killed because they tried to escape, or as part of the disturbing fantasy ritual that Bonnie and Clyde were involved in.

And I wasn't going to figure it out tonight, because it was time to meet Harry.

I finished the last of my, by now stone cold, coffee and headed to the station. He emerged just as I was approaching, blinking in the golden light of the setting sun as it glared directly into his eyes. He shaded them with a hand, his skin tinged pink, a contrast against the pale flame of his amber hair.

"Good timing," I said, falling into step with him on the busy pavement.

"In more ways than one," he agreed. "You don't know how glad I was to get your call. Nothing quite like leaving the office late on a Saturday to go home to an empty flat to make you feel like a loser."

I half-laughed, shaking my head at him. I had the urge to nudge my shoulder against his arm, josh him playfully, but it was a strange feeling. I didn't normally initiate physical contact with others. I held back, unsure of myself. "You're far from being a loser."

"No?" Harry asked, a rueful smile on his face.

"No. I mean, you're not the one hopelessly in love with his best friend – who is actually gay – and yet still can't bring himself to say anything," I said, rubbing a spot on the back of my neck where my hair ended. "That person is surely more of a loser."

"He's not a loser either. Just scared." Harry caught an arm around my shoulders and squeezed for a moment as we walked, before letting it drop. "And his best friend is an arsehole, which probably has something to do with it."

"Look, I know you and Ram…"

"We had a bad experience, and he's not all that bad, and you know all of his good qualities," Harry finished for me. "I know, I know. I just want you to find someone who will be good to you, you know? Coming out to me wasn't easy for you, and I know you have a long road yet to travel. I would like to think that you had people around you to support you on that journey."

"I've got you," I smiled. "One person is a good start."

We paused for a moment, walking down the street past a few other bars to reach our destination. "Why do you call him Ram, anyway?" Harry asked.

"Oh. It's an acronym. Randy Arrogant Muscleman."

Harry snorted with laughter. "That's a good one. You sure it doesn't stand for Really Atrocious Motorbike?"

I laughed along with him. It felt good to poke fun at Ram, even if maybe it wasn't the kindest thing to do. There had been tension between us for a long while, every little thing flaring up into another fight. Letting go of that to laugh, even if he wasn't there, was something I had not realised I needed so badly.

Harry was tapping on his phone screen with a frown as we headed into the bar. "Something wrong?" I asked.

He glanced up, surprised, then stowed his phone away in his jacket pocket. "No, just a text from some idiot I don't fancy talking to right now."

"Fair enough," I said. I paused inside the threshold, letting him take the lead. "Where do you want to sit?"

"There's a table over there," Harry gestured, leading me to more or less the centre of the room, a spot where we would be able to see all around us.

Right in the middle of the room?

I fought down the nervous whine that wanted to tear from my throat and followed him. It was time for me to trust Harry – trust someone other than myself. He knew what he was doing. It wasn't just his experience as an out and proud gay man, but the fact that he had helped and counselled so many others like me, that made me swallow my fear and sit down opposite him.

"You're not comfortable being seen here," he said, thoughtfully, picking up on my apprehension immediately.

"I'm not…" I struggled to articulate it. "I'm not *used* to being seen here. And I… well, I know it's stupid. You don't even have to be gay to come in here. I might just be sitting with a friend, being supportive. And my parents live miles and miles away, and hardly ever even come into London. And if they did, they wouldn't be in a gay bar. And…"

"And yet, you still have this fear that you'll get caught," Harry said. "Follow this train of thought with me. If your parents did see you here, what would happen?"

I swallowed hard, trying to think. "They might ask me what I'm doing here."

"And what would you tell them?"

"I… I don't know." I closed my eyes, looking inside myself for the answer. *Be honest.* "I might lie to them."

"Alright, so in that scenario, they still don't find out that you're gay. Is that terrible?"

"It would be awkward. Lying to their faces."

"So you're letting the fear of a little bit of awkwardness which might, but almost definitely won't, happen, ruin your night?"

I met Harry's eyes with a sheepish laugh. A small quantity of relief flooded through me. He was right, of course. It was stupid to be afraid of something that would never happen. Something that I would be able to handle somehow, if it did.

We sat over our first drinks and chatted, about nothing in particular. The weather, and politics, and the work Harry had been catching up on, and popular TV shows, and anything at all. It was easy and I felt a weight slipping from me. I let my shoulders drop, releasing the tension in them. I even dared to glance around, taking in the faces and figures of those around us.

"Feeling a little better?" Harry asked, when we were onto our second round.

"I am, actually," I said, shaking my head with a sigh. "Earlier today… I wouldn't wish anyone to be involved with this case. It's horrible. You'll know enough, I guess, when it all comes out in the papers."

"I know what it's like," Harry said. "Well, maybe not exactly. But I have students coming to me sometimes with horrific stories. Kids chucked out onto the streets and beaten within an inch of their lives for not being straight or cisgender. Or worse. Those days, I need two things: a stiff drink, and a reminder that not all of humanity is that bad."

That brought a smile to my face. "And today, you're my reminder. I don't know how to thank you for… well, for all of this. For taking my call in the first place, and then actually being supportive."

"Hey, that's what friends are for. And I'm always happy to make a new friend."

I wanted to argue with him, to tell him that it was not as simple as he was making out. That what he had done for me was incredible – something that I never expected anyone to do. But I looked into his face and I saw the way he looked down at his drink, shy of the praise, and I knew that he knew. He just wanted to be modest.

"Me, too," I said, simply. Because he was right. We were friends. And that meant far more to me than he could have guessed.

"So, what's your type, anyway?" Harry asked, changing the subject briskly. "Do you have a type?"

"I don't know," I hummed, tilting my head as I considered it. "I haven't really thought about it."

"Well, who do you find attractive? Other than Julius, I mean."

I searched the wooden surface of the table for answers.

"What about celebrities?" Harry prompted. "Actors, or musicians. There must be someone you've had a bit of a crush on?"

I shook my head wordlessly, spreading my fingers open across the wood and watching them. Nothing came to mind. A celebrity? I always wondered how people could possibly claim to feel genuine attraction to someone like that. You don't even know them. You don't know what they're like. How could it be possible to define attraction to just an image, not a real person?

"Alright, how about this: take a look around the room. Is there someone you find attractive in here?" Harry asked.

I looked around, trying to be subtle. It wasn't easy. Heads turned when I looked around, and I met eyes with a blush that had me catapulting my gaze around to the next person as quickly as I could. By the end of a sweep of the room, I felt exposed, everyone watching me.

"Christ. They think I was watching them," I muttered, lowering my head closer to my glass and trying to hunch over, making myself as small as possible.

Harry smiled gently. "People are just curious," he said. "They're looking for someone to pick up. If you don't look back deliberately and smile at them, they will know it was just a glance."

I cursed, finishing off my lemonade and putting the glass back down harder than I intended. "This is all foreign to me," I said. "I don't know the rules."

"You don't have to follow any," Harry shrugged. "You want another round?"

I nodded my consent as he stood to go to the bar, making sure to keep my eyes downwards. The last thing I wanted was to accidentally flirt with someone.

"Anyway," he said, sliding back in front of me with two fresh glasses. "Did you see anyone you like?"

I shrugged. "It's hard to tell. I don't... I don't know. Just seeing someone, it's..."

I risked a glance up and saw Harry observing me with narrowed eyes. "Just a question," he said. "And don't get defensive, it's just a question. I'm not here to judge. Have you ever felt attraction – I mean, sexual attraction – to anyone but Julius?"

I thought back, desperately tracking through my own mind. I wanted there to be an answer, but there wasn't. There never had been.

"I don't think so," I admitted. "I kind of... tried. When I was at uni, the other guys on my course expected me to come out with them and try to pick up women. I never approached anyone. They put it down to me being shy, but... I already knew I didn't have any interest in women."

"What about men?"

"There was..." My cheeks heated, an unbidden memory of deep embarrassment coming to the surface. "I guess there was one. We were in the same dorm. I used to think about what it would be like to kiss him. But after the first year, we moved apart. After that, I barely even saw him again."

Harry was thoughtfully tapping the side of his glass. "Interesting," he said.

I felt a rising panic circling my chest, squeezing until I could barely get enough air to breathe. "What does that mean?"

Harry looked at me in alarm. "Don't panic, it's nothing bad. I'm just thinking that maybe you only become sexually attracted to someone once you know them a little better."

I buried my head in my arms on the table, letting out a groan. "I told you I'm a loser," I said, my voice muffled by my sleeves. "Twenty-eight years old, and never even been kissed."

"Hey!" I heard Harry's voice move closer, and the chair next to me scraped across the floor a moment before I felt the heat of his arm draped across my shoulders. "You kissed Julius. And anyway, that still doesn't make you a loser. You can't value your worth as a human on what kind of sexual experiences you've had. That's hormonal teenager kind of thinking."

"I might as well be a hormonal teenager," I said, raising my head to look at him. "I haven't ever *done* anything. Don't you think that's pathetic?"

"No, I don't," Harry said. He was half-laughing, but I knew it wasn't at me. He wasn't making fun. There was a warmth that came from him, a genuine care and affection that seeped out of his skin and hovered in the air like perfume. "It's taken you a while to figure out who you are. You're still figuring it out. And that's completely okay. Honestly, you've probably skipped a lot of terrible decisions that you would be regretting by now, like I do."

"Like what?"

"Like the three different girls I had sex with when I was in my late teens, trying to convince myself I could be straight if I just tried," Harry smirked. "Why do you think I'm so good at giving people advice? I've made almost all of the stupid mistakes that anyone makes when they're figuring out if they're gay or not. And I know people – straight people, too – who've chosen to stay virgins until they get married. Not many, admittedly, but they are out there. Usually, it's a religious choice, but some people just feel that sex is something special that should be saved and waited for."

"But I don't feel like that. I just… haven't got around to doing it."

"And how do you feel about that?"

I choked on a chuckle that wanted to break free. "Well, Mr Therapist," I managed. "I feel like I've been wasting the prime of my life. I didn't experiment like you're supposed to in uni. I didn't fool around or make those mistakes. And now when I do end up in a relationship, I'm not going to know what to do."

"Here's a secret: no one knows what to do. Ever. We're all just making it up as we go along." Harry hesitated, then continued. "Look, do you feel like you want to start experimenting now? Trying out those steps towards a relationship?"

I chewed on my lip and scratched my scalp, feeling at once nervous and apprehensive and excited and so many other things I could not name. "Maybe," I conceded. Although doubt flickered through my mind immediately. Harry didn't mean himself, did he?

"You're in a good place to start," Harry said, gesturing around us. "You want to try some flirting? Get someone's number, maybe?"

I breathed deeply, relieved but also slightly horrified by the idea. "Not at all," I said. "But also, yes."

Harry laughed, his eyes glittering. "That's the spirit. There's a guy at the bar who keeps glancing at you, to our left in the red shirt. What do you think about him?"

I looked and caught the man staring right at me, a suggestive smile curving his lips. I turned back to Harry with my cheeks flaming yet again. "Oh, god, I don't know. How am I supposed to know?"

"Objectively, do you think that he is good-looking?"

I thought back, examining my mental image rather than risking more eye contact. The stranger was dark-haired, maybe a little older than me, his frame folded into a sharp suit. He looked like he had maybe come from work to the bar, his tie slightly loosened. He had casually expensive clothing and shoes, worn as if he was nothing, so he earned well; maybe in finance, in the city.

Stop analysing, I told myself.

He had sharp cheekbones, expressive dark eyes, and that hair swept across his forehead in a burst of darkness that framed it all just right. He was, objectively speaking, good-looking. There was no doubt about that.

"Yes," I said. "But I don't know if that means I'm attracted to him."

"For now, you don't have to be," Harry said. "You're just going to talk with him. Flirt a little. It doesn't have to go any further. When you feel like you've gone as far as you want to go, just come back and sit with me. Deal?"

"What if I can't get out of the conversation?" Panic was already filling my throat, closing my airways, constricting my voice.

"Look over here and pretend that I'm waving you over. Tell him you have to go and see what your friend wants."

"Just like that?"

Harry put his hand on top of mine. "Just like that. I promise, if it's too much, I will be here to back you up. We can leave and go to another bar to get away from him. He's not going to push his tongue down your throat the second you start talking to him. Just relax. Why don't you go order us some new drinks? That way you'll have a reason to stand next to him."

I couldn't believe I was doing this. Was I doing it?

"Oh, hell," I muttered, standing up. My legs felt unstable all of a sudden, too jittery to hold me up. I blew out a long breath and forced myself to walk to the bar before I could chicken out, clutching hold of the cold marble countertop edge as if it was the only thing keeping me upright.

I waited for the barman to come over, staring at him desperately, feeling the itching sensation of the stranger watching me from close to my side. I placed our order in a slightly manic tone, too fast, too bright. I was sweating, a cold drip falling down my back.

Then I was waiting for the drinks to be made, standing stock still, too still, shaking, too nervous to look to my right and meet his eye.

I thanked the barman and put my hands on the glasses, making to turn away. I couldn't do it. I couldn't speak to him. This was too much. I –

I turned and met Harry's eyes, and saw his encouraging smile and nod, and screwed mine shut for a moment.

Okay, Will. You can do this.

I made myself look to the right, only to find the stranger still eyeing me with that knowing smile, curving his lips like a bow waiting for an arrow.

"Hi," he said, just one word, his voice silky smooth and amused.

"Um, he- hello," I replied. Whatever the opposite of smooth was, that was me.

There was a pause as he regarded me, his eyes taking their leisurely time to sweep across my face, my shoulders, my chest. "Sitting with your boyfriend?" he asked, at length.

"What? No! Uh, I mean, no. Harry's just a friend."

He was laughing at me with his eyes, the corners crinkling and turning up. "So, you're single."

"I, um, ye-yep. Free as a bird." My voice trailed off as I realised the stupidity of the phrases that were coming out of my mouth. Free as a…? What era was I living in?

The stranger licked his lips, long and slow. "Well, if you get tired of your friend, maybe you should come and have a drink with me instead," he said. "I'm not planning on going anywhere fast."

I ducked my head to the floor, the feeling of the cold glasses in my hands dragging me to reality, distracting my frenzied attempts to think. I didn't want to commit to anything. Nor did I want it to be awkward when we got up and left, and I didn't go over. I didn't want him to wait for me. *Think.*

"We're, ah… this is… you know, I can't just – walk away from – I mean, we made plans," I stammered out, trying to explain, trying to gesture with one of my hands only for a little vodka-tinged lemonade to splash onto my arm. "It would be rude…"

He laughed out loud this time, a throaty, hearty chuckle that came right from the belly. "Relax, twiglet," he said. "Why don't I give you my number? You can call me some other night."

"Some other – right, yes. Yes, that's a good plan." *Twiglet?*

"Do you want me to put it in your phone, or…?"

"Right. Right!" I put the glasses down and hastily grabbed my phone out of my pocket, almost dropping it in the process. It was lucky I had a facial recognition lock set up. There was no way I would have been able to fumble my way through a passcode. I handed it over, watching him type his name and number with ease.

"See you later, then, twiglet," he said with a wink, handing me the phone back. "Don't wait too long to call."

"S-sure," I said, snatching up our drinks again – and spilling more lemonade on myself for my trouble – before stumbling back to Harry, where a third splash of expensive alcohol hit the table.

He was grinning, his face almost split ear to ear. "You did it," he whispered, excitedly.

I nodded, unable to keep the grin from my own face now that I was facing away from the stranger. "I actually did," I agreed. My palms were clammy with sweat and my shirt was sticking to me inside my jumper, and my heart was racing like a rabbit caught in a trap, but I had done it.

And it felt good.

It felt good to be wanted – appreciated – admired. To think that this was a man who would want to have sex with me, strange as it felt to put that sentence together. That I had been measured by his standards and found acceptable, whatever that meant.

"What was his name?" Harry asked.

"Oh, er…" I thumbed through the contacts list on my phone, looking for a name that stood out. It wasn't difficult; the entries were few, and many of those were clients or professional connections. "Selim."

"Well done, Will. How do you feel, now?"

"Weird," I half-laughed. "Good weird. I've got so much adrenaline."

Harry beamed, leaning over the table to slap the side of my arm. "I'm proud of you."

I found myself flushing red again, for the fourth time in an hour or so. "Thanks."

"Now we just need to find *me* a guy." Harry started looking around the bar with exaggerated movements, miming desperation.

"I'm sure you won't have any trouble."

Harry sighed, shaking his head. "With my working hours? I don't know. I need to get out more. Anyway, I'm not really over…"

Ah. The ex. "Sorry. Were you together long?"

Harry shrugged. "A few months. I know, I shouldn't have been so involved, so fast. I tend to fall hard. What can I say? I'm a romantic."

There was a downcast turn to his eyes now that he was thinking about the past, and I didn't like to see it. "Hey, there was something weird," I said, leaning forward and lowering my voice. "He called me twiglet. Is that, like… slang, or something?"

Harry's face creased into a smirk, and he bit his lip, shaking his head with repressed laughter. "Not very down with the kids, are you?"

"What?" I asked. "What does it mean?"

"It doesn't mean anything. Or at least, it isn't some kind of secret gay slang word," Harry reached out and patted my arm through my sleeve. "I think he was just referring to the fact that you look like a stiff breeze could snap you in half."

I looked down at my arm, self-conscious now. Ah, yes. The reason why I didn't like to initiate touching.

"Um, Will," Harry started, his voice quiet and serious now. "I was… well, I wasn't going to bring it up, not yet. But since it has. Are you… apart from all of this, are you alright?"

I swallowed. I studiously examined the glass in front of me, keeping my eyes fixed on that, Harry in my peripheral vision only. "I'm fine. What do you mean?"

As if I didn't know what he meant.

"It's just…" Harry sighed. "This isn't my business, really. I know. You came to me for help with your sexuality, not this. But I see a lot of people who struggle with their identity, and that can manifest in physical ways. Cutting themselves, getting into fights – even… eating disorders."

I was sullen now, the moody teenager again, not wanting to look up or acknowledge the conversation. I stared furiously at the lemonade, watching bubbles slowly break out and move towards the surface. I wouldn't answer. I wouldn't give him that, not for free.

He tried again, all the same. "You're… you're *thin*, Will. I mean, really thin. I can see a difference between now and a few months ago when we first met. I've seen you on Julius' social media accounts before, and you weren't always like this. Something changed this year, didn't it? You've been struggling with food."

I looked up at last, balefully meeting his eyes. "I don't have a problem with food," I said. "I eat as much as I want. I'm in control."

"Alright, alright…" Harry lifted his hands in surrender. "I'm not here to fight with you. I care about your wellbeing, okay? I just… well. I think it would be good for your mental health – even if that has nothing at all to do with your weight and I've got it all wrong – I think it would be good for you to start working your way through this. Coming out. Living your life. You have this burden hanging on your shoulders, dragging you down, stopping you from being who you should be. Pretending to be someone else isn't easy."

"What if I'm not ready?" I asked, the heat draining out of my gaze.

"Then you're not ready," Harry said. "But don't try to wait for a perfect moment, because it will probably never happen. The thing about secrets, especially secrets we have guarded closely for a long time, is that it's hard to let them go. Come out when you feel like you can handle it. I'm not saying you should rush into it – it's your life and your decision. But I've seen too many people choked back by this toxic lie of a life, wasting their potential, to let you do the same without saying a thing."

"It's funny," I said, giving him a wry smile. "In my line of work, what we usually say is that secrets always come out in the end."

"Better to be the one in control of the narrative," Harry said, knocking back the last of his drink. "Not the one scrambling to put their life back together after an unexpected push."

18 – RAM

Everything is a blur.

There are noises, but too many for my head to make sense of. Echoing near, far, loud, shrill, low and close, urgent. Voices. I can't make out individual words. I pry my eyes open to lights, too bright, too many, and shadows crowding in around me.

I close them again, and shut it all out, wanting only the darkness.

At first, I keep my eyes closed. That is the best way to go about this. Keep them closed, don't look, don't see. Don't see what you've done to yourself this time.

I know where I am. It's not hard to work out. I can hear the steady beeping of machines around me, the heartrate monitor letting everyone know that I am still alive. The soft touch of a bed underneath my body, though not so soft and comfortable that I could possibly mistake it for my own. A smell hanging in the air, like disinfectant and sanitiser gel, and the occasional cough or shuffle from ahead or to the sides.

There is something on my face – around my nose and mouth, delivering me oxygen. I can feel the texture of a duvet cover on my lower legs, but not my body. Something papery and scratching fills the space between.

And something warm on my hand – something that moves slightly every now and then, almost imperceptibly. Something through which I can feel a heartbeat which is out of time with the steady beeping of my monitors.

I inventory my body: feet, legs, knees, hips, stomach. All seem fine. Back, arms and hands, shoulders, head. The only thing I can feel is a small, pinching sensation in my right hand, and that warm weight on top of it.

I peel my eyes open slowly, wincing and closing them again after the bright light hits me. My head is thumping with pain, needles piercing right down through my irises and into the back of my skull. I try again, slower this time, every tiny movement of my eyelashes allowing that much more in, until I can at least see clearly – even if it still sends pain ricocheting off the insides of my brain.

I flick my gaze down and to the right and I see – just as I know I will – Will. He is watching me closely, but not my face; his attention is on my hand where he clasps it against the bedsheet, and I know he has not yet realised I am awake.

I search his face for a short moment, taking stock. He looks tired, his face etched deep with lines of worry. But he isn't wearing the clothes I last saw him in. More to the point, he is illuminated by natural light, coming through from a window above and behind my bed. It is daytime. It must be the day after I left the house, went out to a bar, and saw him with Harry.

Ah. Harry.

The events of the night before start to flood back into place. The bar, the drinks. The feelings of loneliness and rejection compounded by the pretty little thing who knocked me back. Two bottles of whiskey multiplying into more until I lost count altogether.

And now a hospital bed, with Will hunched over me like he is worried I might not wake up after all.

I stir guiltily, letting him know I am awake. Instantly his expression changes to open concern, as he leaps to his feet and calls a nurse from the other end of the room. I hear her footsteps pattering across the linoleum floor.

"You're back with us, Mr Rakktersen," she says. She stands on her tiptoes to peer into my eyes, checking my oxygen mask, the saline drip attached to a needle in the back of my hand. "How are you feeling?"

I reach up to pull the mask out of the way, easing a dry tongue against a dry mouth. "Sore," I say. "I could do with some water."

"That does not surprise me," she says, her hands busy with things I cannot keep track of. "Would you like to sit up?"

At my assent, she lifts the back of the bed, helping me to prop myself up into a sitting position on the newly curved surface. Then she hands me a glass of water poured efficiently from a jug and watches while I drink it.

"Are you aware of what happened to you, Mr Rakktersen?"

I look at the bed, the saline, my body in a hospital robe. "I get the feeling that I happened to me," I say.

Her lips quirk into a smile for only the briefest second before she has it under control again. "You did indeed," she says. "You were brought in last night, unconscious and suffering the effects of alcohol poisoning. As the effects were very severe, we had to perform a gastric lavage – that's a stomach pump – and put you on fluids."

"Shit." I close my eyes as her words sink in. I could have done serious damage to myself.

"You're extremely lucky that a member of staff at a bar spotted you. They were closing up and saw you passed out in a doorway. If it wasn't for their quick thinking, you may well have succumbed either to the alcohol poisoning or the cold last night."

I open my eyes again and see Will, looking right at me. His eyes are brimming with tears, swimming until he stubbornly blinks them away. He looks like he doesn't know whether to be relieved or furious. I can't say I blame him.

"What time is it?" I ask.

The nurse checks the watch attached to the front of her uniform. "Twelve thirty," she says. "You're just in time for lunch. I'd recommend eating the whole plate. Your body needs the nutrients."

She disappears, off on her rounds to see another patient, leaving me some breathing space. Though not much. Will is still here, and by the glower he is giving me, I'm not his favourite person right now.

"What a way to find out you listed me as your next of kin," he says, at last.

I can't help but break into a smile, even if the sudden movement makes me wince. "I figured my roommate would be the most useful person to have around in the event of an emergency. What do my parents know about me that you don't?"

"How to deal with you, maybe," Will says. He sinks back into the chair at my side, running a hand over his face.

That's fair, but it still hurts. "Sorry," I say. "I know it's not enough to just fucking say it, but I can't do much else right now."

"Why are you sorry to me?"

"Because I made you worry."

Will gives a short, sharp sigh, an exasperated and angry noise that has me snapping my head up. The action makes my brain feel like it is rocking inside my skull, and I grip a fistful of the bedclothes until it steadies.

"Me being worried is not the most serious thing that happened here," he says, staring furiously, for some reason, at my knees. "You heard the nurse. You could have died last night."

I draw in a deep breath. "I heard."

"That's it?"

"I…" I throw my hands in the air, wincing again at the pull on the skin of my hand as the needle jerks the tube around. "No, that's not it. I realise how stupid this was. How dangerous. I just don't know what you want me to say."

"What I want doesn't come into it. If I had what I wanted, we would be waking up to a normal Sunday morning and bickering over what to binge-watch tonight, not waiting for you to get discharged from hospital."

I offer him a small smile. "We don't bicker," I say.

"No, you're right. You dictate what we can and can't do, I try to protest, and I get shot down, and we do what you want to do anyway." Will slumps back in his chair, his arms folded over his chest.

Alright. So we're not in a joking mood.

Will was already pissed at me before, and this will hardly have made things any better. I need to enter damage control, and I need to do it fast before he leaves and there's nothing more I can do.

"I didn't mean..." I sigh, then shake my head and start again. "I lost control. I did. I don't know what came over me."

"Nothing came over you." Will stares at me sullenly, meeting my gaze. "You are an alcoholic, Ram. You were binge drinking. Like alcoholics do."

His words hit me square in the chest.

The worst part of it is that I know he's fucking right.

I close my eyes and tip my head back against the pillows. "Okay," I say, ashamed of the way my voice cracks in the middle of the word.

"Okay?"

I bite my lip, swallowing down the lump in my throat. "I'm..."

I can't think of a good way to end the sentence. I can't think of anything. He's right. I am an alcoholic. I've never even admitted that to myself before. I've always seen myself as in control, able to stop whenever I wanted. But I'm not. Last night proved that, if a hundred other nights before it didn't.

"Are you going to tell me I'm wrong?"

I ease my eyes open to look at Will, to allow him to see me. To exchange meaning in a way that only eyes can, and words cannot express. "No," I say, hoarse not just from the dryness of my throat.

He seems to soften a little at that, something of the anger in his expression melting away.

But it shouldn't. He should be angry with me. He should be furious. This is all my fault. I'm the one that pushed us to go to the US. I'm the one that got us into trouble out there, forcing us to run back home with our tails between our legs. I'm the one who couldn't fucking handle Will having so much as a friendship with someone else, and had to use it as an excuse to drink myself into oblivion.

I scrub my hands across my face quickly, wiping the tears away.

"I'm just…" I search for words, and find and grasp hold of the ones that ring most true. "I'm just really glad you're here."

"We have to get you some help," Will says, and the mixture of both relief and fear inside me boils in my stomach like a nest of vipers.

NINETEEN – WILL

I didn't think I had ever been that worried before in my life.

Worried was not even the term for it. I was once worried about whether I would pass my A-Levels. I used to be worried about not finding a job I wanted to do after university. I've been worried about whether I remembered to lock the door or turn the oven off.

Those sensations were nothing, absolutely nothing, compared to this.

It was more like primal fear, utter nervous terror at the thought that Ram might die. Getting woken up by a call in the early hours of the morning from the hospital, with a calm-voiced nurse informing me that Julius Rakktersen had been brought in by paramedics and was about to undergo a procedure, was one of the most awful moments of my life up to that point.

Perhaps not the very worst, but an extremely close contender.

Then waiting for hours in a sterile room with chairs thronged by emergency patients and their families and friends, watching people receiving both good news and bad from doctors with deep black bags under their eyes. I had to sit and wait for word until official visiting hours began, and then, at last, they allowed me in to sit by his bedside.

That only began a long and anxious vigil for him to wake up.

I had never seen him like that. His face was sallow, his hair greasy, swept back onto his pillow. He didn't look asleep – not resting, peacefully. He looked drained and ill and older than I remembered, as if he had aged overnight. Maybe he had. Stress on the body can do that to you.

And yet still, despite all of that, he was Ram. That bone structure, his strong jaw and noble, straight nose. That rock star aura that seemed to hang off him, that was more than the leather jackets and tattoos and jewellery – that made him look like a fallen angel even now, at his worst.

The longer I sat watching him, the angrier I became. Angry that he had risked his life, that it had finally come to this. Angry at myself for letting it go this far before forcing him to get help, believing him when he said that he was in control. He wasn't in control. He hadn't been in control for a long time.

I was angry that we had fought, the day before, and that our last memory together might have been something like that. I was angry that I had finally made some progress on myself, started to accept who I was and have a good time with a new friend, and Ram had to ruin it by getting himself in hospital. I was angry that any of this was happening to either of us at all, that it wasn't fair, that we hadn't known what we were getting ourselves into back then.

The nurse ordered me to go and get breakfast on her morning rounds. It felt good to surrender to someone else, to just do as I was told. I ate dull porridge laced with sweet strawberry jam, the stodgy texture never quite allowing them to fully mix, and returned to him.

And even though I was relieved when he finally woke up, there was a heavy weight of anger just waiting to crash down through the opening of the dam.

What I wasn't expecting was for him to accept it, to own his part in all of this. To simply close his eyes and put his head back instead of arguing with me.

"I'm just…" he said, looking at me with a raw and honest vulnerability that I had never seen before. "I'm just really glad you're here."

And how was I supposed to stay mad at him, after that?

"We have to get you some help," I told him. "Get you into a program, or something. You can't carry on like this."

"Yeah," he agreed, and even though normally I would have wanted more of a promise, I let it go. It was all there in the inflection, in the heaviness of his voice, the sag of his shoulders.

The hospital lunch delivery interrupted us, a cart bearing various trays entering the room at the hands of a tall man in a blue uniform. He deposited one of them in front of Ram after a brief quiz about his dietary requirements and a check of his chart, and then went on his way. I left Ram staring at the dismal, brown mess in dismay to find a vending machine or some kind of snack.

I lucked out in a café that was the opposite direction to the dreary cafeteria I had visited that morning, a national chain brand with sandwiches and pastries on offer. I joined Ram again with a sandwich and a coffee, and pushed a pain au chocolat onto his tray when no one was looking.

"We have a lot to talk about," I said, wiping the last crumbs away from the corners of my mouth.

Ram sighed. "I'm feeling a bit better. Maybe they'll let me go home tonight."

I shook my head. "The nurse said you were staying in overnight for further observation. Which means that you're trapped here, and can't get away from me. Get it?"

Ram lay his head back against his propped-up pillows, eyeing me with a weary and resigned expression. "I get it. No escape. Better do as I'm told."

I pressed my lips together for a moment, trying to find a way to express my disapproval of that statement without snapping his head off and proving his point. "Not just as you're told. I need you to be honest with me."

Ram nodded. "I can do honest. At least, I can try."

"I need you to do more than try – much more," I insisted. "The thing is, Ram, we've got to get to the bottom of this. The reason why you can't stop drinking. The thing that pushed you into a hospital bed. If we don't deal with this, it could end up killing you."

Ram looked as though he was going to disagree, raising his hand slightly. The motion tugged on the IV line still attached to his hand, and he closed his mouth, then his eyes. "You're right," he said at last. "We just kept putting it off. But I guess it's time."

"It's time we talk about San Francisco," I agreed, dragging my chair closer to the top of the bed so that we could speak without being overheard.

20 – RAM

My body is a strange thing that may or may not actually still be attached to my consciousness. The aching has faded away after they gave me a dose of painkillers, until it is just a buzz at the edge of my hearing. Something I can easily ignore. And for the rest, it's hard to believe that a few hours ago I was undergoing some kind of procedure to get the poison out of my body.

The poison that I deliberately and knowingly put into it.

And despite all of this, when Will brings up San Francisco, all I can feel is a desperate and fervent wish that I had a bottle of whiskey to see me through it.

This is not going to be comfortable. Not at all. And I have to endure it not only sober, but beyond sober – heading into withdrawal with a long day ahead of sitting in hospital with wires coming out of my skin.

"I've been an idiot," I say, twitching my hand and moving the IV line up and down. "I shouldn't have let it get this far."

"I should have said something when I saw you going down this path," Will sighs. "I knew things weren't right. But it was too painful to talk about, so I never brought it up."

"You knew I was drinking to shut it out. I didn't want to deal with it. I didn't want to think about it at all."

"That's not an excuse. I should have forced you to listen."

"Nobody forces me to do anything." I manage a small grin. "My dad found that out the hard way."

Will forces a laugh, shaking his head. "But you don't need to feel like an idiot. We're both in this together. We both made mistakes that could have been prevented. What's important now is putting them right."

"I still feel like a chump." I chew on rough skin on my lower lip, trying to think of a way forward. I don't want to talk about this. I actually don't. But I think Will is right – we have to.

"So. San Francisco."

I meet Will's eyes and see them brimming with fear and nerves and the trepidation of a subject that will be painful for both of us. I close mine so that I don't have to see them. Will in pain is the last thing I have ever wanted to see.

"San Francisco," I repeat.

"It was… traumatic, for both of us."

"I get these…" I swallow hard, remembering how it felt to watch the Highgate Strangler with his hands around Will's throat. How I hesitated for a moment, my head full of a different night, a different city. "I don't know, I guess flashbacks. Sometimes, I hear something or I see something, and – I'm back there."

I feel Will's fingers curling around mine, and open my eyes in surprise. He is looking down at our intertwined hands, a frown creasing his brow. "Me, too. I think about it constantly."

"You don't deserve that. It wasn't your fault. None of it was."

"Of course it was my fault!" Will's gaze flies to mine, indignant. "How can you pretend that it wasn't?"

"It wasn't," I say.

"A man is d-" Will stops himself, glances around hurriedly, and leans in closer to hiss in a quieter tone. "A man is dead, and it was my bullet that killed him. It couldn't be more my fault."

I shake my head in disbelief. "What are you talking about? *I* fired the first shot. I hit him first."

We stare at each other for a long moment, the idle sounds of the room the only interruption. Someone two beds down coughs and Will pinches the bridge of his nose before running a hand back through his hair.

"You're wrong," he says. "I've been over it, over and over again in my head. I pulled the trigger before I heard your shot. I know I did."

"It was the opposite way round," I growl. "I pulled the trigger, then heard *your* shot. I've known that since the moment it happened. I haven't gone over the memory until it changed. I knew it was me right away."

"My memory hasn't changed," Will hisses at me. "Don't patronise me. It won't help."

"I'm not -" I sighed, cutting myself off. "I'm being serious. You did nothing wrong."

"I did something wrong," Will replied darkly. "I shot an innocent man. Whatever the outcome, that was never going to be right."

We pause again, his words sinking in, soaking the whole room around us. I can't argue with that. Even if he had lived, we would have been in a lot of trouble.

"I just can't understand," Will says, his voice choking off and forcing him to start again. "I can't understand how we got it that wrong. We did all the investigative work. There were so many clues, so many signs."

"He looked guilty as sin. You know he did. I don't... I don't know how they managed to set him up so well. Make everything point in his direction. They couldn't have known that we would..."

"That we would chase him. And that he would run," Will finishes for me. "Even though he hadn't done anything wrong. Why did he run?"

"Maybe because we were pointing guns at him," I say, sighing and rubbing a hand stubbornly across my eyes, refusing to let anything leak out. "Maybe because he knew how bad it looked. I guess he thought he could get away from us, go somewhere safe, and prove his innocence."

I remember the wild look in his eyes. Special Agent Kit Anderson, turning to face us on a rooftop, the wind blowing back through his hair and sending his coat billowing behind him. The way he reached into his shoulder holster, his hand already gripping the barrel of his weapon.

And me, without a moment of hesitation or doubt, firing before he had a chance to do the same to us.

Before he could turn and shoot me, or Will, because I couldn't tolerate that. All of our training had prepared us to prevent that. And I had always been good at learning new things.

"I can't… I can't get that look out of my head," I whisper. "The way he looked at us. Down at his chest, at the blood, and then…"

"And then he looked at us like we'd killed him. Because we had."

"Both shots right to the chest. Through and out. He wouldn't have had much chance of surviving either of them."

Will looks down at our hands again, wetting his lips, thinking carefully. "It wouldn't have mattered," he says. "If you shot first, or I did. If only one of us did. He was dead from either shot."

"But it was me. It wasn't you. I'm the one who killed him."

Will meets my eyes, a tear spilling over and running down his cheek, a track that I cannot reach out to trace. "It doesn't matter. Don't you see what I'm saying? He was dead either way. So it doesn't matter who shot first. We both – we *both* killed him."

Again, I find myself unable to argue with him. As he always does, Will has wrapped me in logic I can't cut through. Tied up with a knot that can't be broken. If I shot first, then I killed him. But if I hadn't shot at all, then Will's bullet still would have done the job.

We're both guilty.

"Sometimes I think we should have stayed and told them what we'd done," I say. The unbearable thought has my voice cracking. "Owned up to it and faced the music. Gone to fucking jail, maybe. Paid for it."

"It wouldn't have made a difference. Not to us. He was dead either way. And the agency protects its own."

"But we didn't pay for it," I insist. "No one did. Kit's family – they all think -"

Will shushes me, looking around again. No one seems to be looking in our direction. Most of the residents of the room are elderly and sleeping. "Don't use his name. Just in case."

"They all think he was murdered by some criminal," I continue. "Someone who will never be caught. They're never going to get closure."

"He was an FBI agent. There's danger in the job. He wasn't just a civilian. His family knew that."

"So that makes it alright?"

Will's eyes brim with tears again, falling down his cheeks to patter quietly onto the bed between us. "Of course it doesn't make it alright. I'm just... I'm just trying to make you feel better."

"You might be fighting a losing battle there." I give him a wry smirk, no real warmth or humour in it. "I shouldn't feel better. I don't fucking deserve to feel better."

"You wouldn't have felt better in prison."

"I might have."

"No, you wouldn't. You would have had to look his family in the eyes – all of them. Seen them in court. Repeated the whole story over and over again. And no matter what sentence they gave us, it wouldn't have been enough."

"Us," I repeat, squeezing his fingers lightly. "That's the only part of all of this that makes me feel remotely okay. Human. The fact that if I had gone down for this, you would have too. I wanted to protect you from that."

"That's why you thought of picking up the bullets," Will says, his voice barely louder than a breath. He is looking down, and I know what he is seeing: not the hospital floor, but the rooftop, the darkness, hunting for spent ammunition by the light of our phones.

"The only real evidence that we had anything to do with it. It was sheer luck that both rounds passed through his body and out the other side. Sheer luck that we could find them before the local police arrived on the scene."

"Not luck," Will shook his head. "Design. The standard FBI weapons at our disposal. Only the best."

"And it was luck that they believed us when we told them we had to get out of the country through grief. That we were just these sappy English pacifists who fled at the first hint of gun violence. Not used to it. That we didn't grow up in their trigger-happy culture and couldn't handle it when we were exposed to it for the first time."

"It was true enough. I've felt sick every time I've thought about guns since then. The way all I had to do was fire off a single shot, and he just crumpled, falling, hitting the floor..."

I squeeze Will's hand again to get his attention, to stop him from spiralling down. "It made me feel powerful," I confessed. "When we... when you were being... with the Highgate Strangler. I wanted a gun then. I wanted to fucking shoot him."

"You thought he was going to kill me. That's different."

The thought of losing Will, now as it did then, fills me with dread. An overwhelming wave of emotion is threatening to drown me. All of the things I have been tuning out this past year – trying to ignore and run away from. To talk about them like this is somehow both cathartic and threatening. I don't know how much more I can handle.

"He was a colleague," I say, jumping back in the conversation, knowing that Will will follow me. "Someone we should have mourned. We never mourned him."

"We did it in our own ways."

"No. I mourned for myself," I say, catching Will's eye. He almost jumps back at the fire and rage I have discovered inside of myself, the bitter anger at the person I have made myself into. "I felt sorry for myself. Like a whining fucking narcissist. I burned my career. Threw everything away. Just like my fucking dad said I would. I was selfish. Self-centred."

"We ran," Will says. "Nothing more selfish than that."

"Not far enough."

There's a pause, and then I add: "How do we ever get over this?"

"I don't think we do," Will says. "We shouldn't. He deserves that we remember him. That we are punished for his death, one way or another."

"I keep thinking," I swallow hard, the lump in my throat hard to talk around. "I keep thinking that if we just save enough people _"

"One more." It almost breaks my heart to hear him agree with me. "Always, just one more."

I look at Will, at the ghost of himself that he has become. So frail that I worry I will snap his fingers when I squeeze them. And me, lying in a hospital bed, only saved because I passed out in public and one person decided not to simply step over me. Frankly, he probably just wanted me off his property and out of his conscience. I have been trying so hard to destroy myself that I almost succeeded.

"I'm sorry," I say, my voice failing me, and when I say that I mean everything: I'm sorry for getting it so wrong, I'm sorry for shooting Kit Anderson, I'm sorry for dragging you out there and then making us both run away, I'm sorry for not talking to you, I'm sorry for getting jealous over a kiss that meant nothing, I'm sorry for drinking myself nearly to death.

Will can only meet my eyes for a moment, and he ducks his head down to the covers of the bed, and says nothing. His shoulders begin to shake, and I realise he is crying, and the only thing I can do is rest my free hand on the back of his head and hope it provides some form of comfort. I close my eyes and let the tears come, silently, moving through me like water, like a tap turned on. I don't move, even though Will's shoulders shake up and down with the strength and depth of his emotion. I don't move at all.

TWENTY-ONE - WILL

"Ready to go?" I asked. The false cheer in my voice was so brittle that it felt like a small breeze could shatter it, but Ram simply nodded and stood up.

He had been perched on the edge of his bed when I arrived, already dressed and groomed, a little paler than usual but otherwise no worse for wear. The small pharmacy bag he carried alongside the duffel of his clothes was the only real indication that anything had happened at all.

Yesterday had been a lot to deal with. A lot of emotions I had fought with for a long time, finally brought to the surface and released, and yet I couldn't quite say that I felt better. Sharing responsibility was not much better than being the sole perpetrator. A breakthrough that came at the expense of Ram nearly dying was hardly something to celebrate.

"I brought the rental car," I said, as we walked through the corridor. The floor was so smooth that my trainers squeaked. "Figured that would be nicer than the Tube."

Ram nodded quietly. "Good thinking."

"I told Alex that we won't be back in the station until tomorrow."

"Why did you do that?"

I caught a flash of anger in Ram's eyes when I glanced at him, but he was already looking away. He strode towards the main waiting area and the exit, evidently keen to get out of this place.

"We have things to deal with," I said.

Ram made a frustrated noise, pushing his hair out of his forehead with a hand still bearing a plaster from the IV line. "Yesterday was – it was enough. I don't want to talk about it anymore. Not right now."

"I don't mean that," I said. "I need to… look, can we just wait until we get home? I don't want to get into it here."

I didn't want to get into it at all, really. Except I did. And I didn't. I yo-yoed back and forth in my head so many times that I hardly knew whether I was coming or going. All I did know was that Harry was right – about most things, actually. But most of all, he was right about what my next course of action needed to be.

Ram stormed ahead of me to the car, ignoring my words and pushing past people to get out. We crossed the car park in silence, and he waited for me in the passenger seat as I paid the exorbitant charge to leave.

I switched the radio on to fill the silence, but almost immediately grimaced and turned it off. Some overpaid talk show host jabbering on about their own lives instead of actually playing music. Not that I was usually much interested in the kind of music that got played during the day. Over the past few years, it had begun to feel like I was losing touch with what the rest of the nation apparently enjoyed listening to. Maybe that was what happened the closer you got to thirty.

We stopped at a set of traffic lights, and I hastily flicked through apps on my phone, setting up a podcast to play through the speakers. Another cold case report, the kind of thing I liked to listen to, challenging myself to solve it. Not that it was ever that easy. Usually, a cold case is cold because the evidence just isn't there – or because they already know who did it and just can't make it stick in court. In which case, the crime has really already been solved anyway.

The narrator went into detail describing a grisly murder scene, and how the parents of the victim had been the first ones to stumble across it, and Ram reached over to switch off the sound with a vicious motion.

I spared him the longest glance I could before looking back at the road, but he was surly and silent, staring stonily ahead. His arms were folded across his chest, his head tilted towards the passenger side window. There was no invitation for talk or further listening in that expression.

I tapped my fingers nervously on the steering wheel as we paused in traffic. The last thing I needed right now was silence. I needed to focus on something, anything, other than what I needed to say next.

I watched the cars ahead, counting off their colours. Grey, red, red, blue, grey, black, red, blue, grey, grey – beyond that, unseen. Shops on the side of the road. Barber, florist, off-license, café, café, electronics. People walking past. Man. Man. Dog. Woman. Man – *no, stop this. Stop spiralling.*

I began humming under my breath, a stupid little tune I remembered from my childhood. Funny that it was the first thing that came to mind, but I needed something to settle my thoughts. I could feel myself spiralling down into panic. I couldn't do that – not right now.

I didn't really know how I made it back to our road, where I could concentrate on pulling up on the kerb and parking. I knew that Ram was about ready to snap, between my tapping and humming, the nervous knee-jiggling that began every time we had to wait to move forward. It was hardly a secret that he was annoyed with me. He exuded it like a cloud around him, sharp looks that made me pause for a moment each time until my nerves got the better of me and I had to start it all again.

As soon as we got into the flat, Ram started to push past me, heading in the direction of his room. I could so clearly see it: he would disappear in there and slam the door, then refuse to come out and talk to me. He thought I still wanted to dredge up the past. This wasn't about that.

I put a hand out to stop him, my fingers splaying on his chest. "Just wait, please. It's… it's about me. Not Kit. Please, just sit down."

Ram sighed heavily. "Is this what it's going to be like now? You trying to guilt trip me into deep and meaningfuls?"

A pang hit my chest. "It's not like that. I've got something to tell you. Just sit?"

Ram blew out a heavy sigh of frustration, then took a seat on the couch. He had a wild, aggressive look about him, like a rebellious teenager who was ready for a fight from the moment a conversation began. It wasn't the environment I had hoped for, for my big confession. It wasn't something that I had hoped for at all.

I sat next to him, carefully, almost primly, balanced on the edge of the seat. My back was straight, my shoulders set. Still, I could only look at my hands when I began speaking. "Harry's been giving me some advice. He's been pushing me to do something, and I have to admit that he was right."

Ram shifted towards me, alarm blaring through his body. "Oh, fucking fantastic. Harry? Don't tell me, he's convinced you that you need to move out and stop working with me."

I risked a look up and saw that Ram was not as full of anger and buffeting energy as he pretended. Fear was written across his features instead. He genuinely still thought that Harry was trying to come in-between us.

"That's not it," I said, softly. "Actually, Harry's been… a real friend. But it's not about him."

"Then what?" Ram demanded, still surly to hide his anxiety.

I cleared my throat once, then forced my mouth to open up and say it. I couldn't beat around the bush anymore. I couldn't let myself delay or find an excuse to put this off. It had to be now, and today, before the moment was gone and we were no longer getting things off our chests.

Nerves constricted my throat, almost swallowed my tongue. I had to say it now. I had to force my mouth to move, my lips to form the words – why was it so hard?

I looked down at my own hands, closed my eyes for a bare second, and took a breath. Then I said it, all at once, a rush of breath before I could shut down again.

"I'm gay."

The words made me feel sick to my stomach and light as a feather all at once. I had finally said it out loud – finally told him.

But his expression was pure confusion, not the acceptance that I had been hoping for.

"Wait – but…" he started, then shook his head, his eyes slowly widening as what I had said hit home.

"I haven't accepted it within myself for a long time," I said. "To tell the truth, it was the Strangler case that made me confront it head-on. Being in that environment and still having to hide who I was. It was beginning to make less and less sense."

"But all this time…"

I swallowed, my whole body trembling. "I'm sorry," I said. "I know it should have been easy to tell you. Of all people. I mean, it's not like I've been afraid of you judging me for it. But I didn't want it to be true. I wanted to be… the good, normal son that my parents wanted. Not – not *different*."

Ram looked away from me for a moment, processing. My heart jumped in my chest. Could I have been wrong? Was he going to reject me, like I had always been afraid of everyone else doing? I thought he was the one person above all who would get it – would accept it without a moment of doubt. Was I wrong?

Were things between us going to change forever, now that he knew I must have meant it when I kissed him?

"And that's all it is?" Ram asked, unexpectedly, his head swinging back towards me. "Genuinely? Harry's just been helping you to decide whether to come out?"

"There's no 'just' about it, from where I've been sitting. But yes."

Ram heaved a huge sigh of relief and leaned forward to pull me into a brief hug. "Thank fuck. You know I don't care about things like that. You're Will, same as you've ever been. I guess it explains why you haven't had a girlfriend all this time, but that's all. I'm happy for you. You can start really living as yourself now."

"Well, sort of," I said. As soon as the warmth of his body left mine, I wished for it back. "I still haven't told my parents. And I don't know if I will."

"That's a bridge we can cross later," Ram said. The way that it was already 'we' made something in the region of my stomach flip and turn, a giddiness and gratitude at the fact that Ram was still the same best friend I could rely on. "Why couldn't you come to me first? Why did it have to be Harry?"

I could sense that he was hurt. "I couldn't put my finger on it at first. I just knew that he was someone I could trust. Later I found out he does this for a living. He's been helping LGTBQ students since he was at uni himself. I guess he has a knack for it."

"Shit." Ram dug his phone out of his pocket. "I think I owe him an apology. I might have accused him of trying to poison you against me."

"When?"

"Saturday night." He had the decency to look embarrassed. "When I was drinking."

While Ram fired off a message to Harry, biting his lip and then his thumbnail as he hemmed over the wording, I watched him with a kind of curious feeling. He had seemed so relieved when I told him my big announcement. What was that? Was he just glad I wasn't actually ditching our friendship because of Harry? Or maybe the fact that he had someone to share things with now – that we were the same? I couldn't figure him out. As much as I could read his mind sometimes, at other times I might as well have been looking at a stranger.

"Tell me something," Ram said, looking up at last and putting his phone away. His gaze ducked, down somewhere around the hem of my jumper, as if he couldn't bear to meet my eyes just then. "Was it… sort of… triggered by the, um. The kiss?"

My heart caught in my throat at the fact that he would bring it up. A flame lit up my cheeks, and my voice almost stuck behind it before I found my composure enough to answer. "No. I've known for a long time. Inside, anyway. I just thought that maybe if I ignored it for long enough, it wouldn't be real anymore."

A brief smile passed over his face. "If that worked, it would be a much smaller community. Almost all of us have probably wished at some point that we could pray it away, or ignore it, or just find the strength to change ourselves."

"I know it's not that easy now," I said. "And it feels right, saying it out loud. I am what I am, what I've always been. I don't want to pretend anymore."

"So are you coming out, like coming out?" Ram quirked an eyebrow. "To everyone?"

I rubbed that spot at the back of my head that always itched whenever something felt awkward. "I don't think so," I said. "Nobody really needs to know. I guess you do, because we live together, and everything else. But if it doesn't affect someone, they don't need to know. It doesn't matter whether I'm straight or gay."

"I can't tell if you're being very mature, or just trying to avoid talking about it," Ram said, his normal grin returning finally to light up his eyes. "But I'll respect that. And if you change your mind about anything, then we can talk about it again. What do you want me to do if someone asks me outright?"

"I don't see why anyone would."

"Maybe we're in a bar, and someone wants to chat you up, and they check with me first to see if you're available."

The idea of him helping to set me up with someone else stung. I guessed that, even if I was out in the open now, it changed nothing between us. He really was not interested in me. Not like that.

"Then you can tell them, I guess. Just… just not my parents. I don't know how the Ambassador would take it."

"Do you ever get tired of calling your own father that?" Ram asked, a change of direction that caught me off guard.

"That's who he is."

"Yes, but he's your father. Your dad. Even I call mine Dad, and he's not exactly been a model parent."

I shrugged. "It wasn't like that, when I was growing up. He was the Ambassador. That's what everyone called him. Anyway, look. I've already made one big confession today. Can we leave unravelling our own respective daddy issues for another day?"

Ram quirked a smile and nodded. "I need some good solid food, after that hospital sludge. Will you kill me if I order a takeaway? We can have it for lunch, save the leftovers for tea."

I thought about the past twenty-four hours. About the confessions made, the fear for Ram, the progress towards healing. Talking about Kit brought it all to the fore again, and stirred up all those nasty, sick feelings of guilt that were always eating away at me. But maybe we had done enough, just in that little moment there, to justify some small kind of reward.

"I won't kill you," I said. "But no pineapple on the pizza or I might have to reconsider."

22 – RAM

"Glad you could join us," Alex says, a heavy dose of sarcasm lading down his tone.

He looks even more tired than he did the last time we saw him. I wonder if he's taken any time off at all, over the last three days.

"I would have been here sooner if I could," I say, pointedly. "The nurses wouldn't let me get out of bed."

A flicker of guilt passes through Alex's eyes. "Sorry. I'm just trying to catch these sick bastards. We need all hands on deck. I don't mind admitting that I need as much help as I can get on this one."

The lights of a police car, setting off nearby and flashing red and blue, pass over Alex's worn features as the driver leaves the car park. The flashes of colour intersect with the dull yellow of the streetlight above us, which washes out his complexion entirely. His tie is slightly crooked, and his chin bears at least two days' stubble.

"We're here now," Will says, popping up at my side. "What's the briefing?"

"You've missed a lot," Alex begins, but then sighs. "And yet, not very much at all. We put out an appeal for information on Simon Shystone, but worded it carefully – not wanting to alert them that we're on their trail. We managed to get lucky. We had an eye-witness report, since confirmed by CCTV, that put Shystone in Shoreditch when he was last seen. Apparently, he was on a night out that he hadn't told anyone about. Which means he wasn't snatched in Kent at all, and this case is firmly ours."

"Do we know where Riley was taken from? I mean, originally, before he went to Kent?"

"We have some idea. Put together with the two victim statements that we do have, we've managed to narrow down the area where we think Bonnie and Clyde are operating. Shoreditch, Spitalfields, Hackney. It doesn't allow us to narrow down on a specific area or street, but we believe this is where they are taking their victims from."

I nod my chin towards the groups of plain-clothed police officers, men and women heading out in unmarked cars in twos and threes. "And you're putting people in strategic locations to try and catch them in the act."

"This may not yield anything at all, of course," Alex says, folding his arms across his chest. He is wearing a dark, long coat over a black jumper – his version of casual wear, which somehow makes him look even more like a copper. "For all we know, they have a victim already strapped to their chair. In that case, I doubt we'll see anything until they release them. But we've been given a couple of weeks to try this with some reinforcements, so we've got to give it a go."

"What's the plan, then?" Will asks.

Alex turns back to the map he has spread out over the bonnet of his car. "We've got people loosely stationed at each of these red markers," he said. They were spread across natural distances, places where they might be able to more or less keep one another in sight. "Some are dressed normally in casual clothes and will take the role of bystanders. Smokers, pretending to be on phone calls, waiting for someone, and so on. We've got some female officers posing as sex workers, and some of our male officers will also be posing as Johns – either going up to our own plants, or to the real thing, with visible wedding rings."

"Being the kind of victims that Bonnie and Clyde like to go for," I conclude.

"Exactly. We'll be performing miniature plays, of a sort. Approach the woman, organise a tryst, go off into a dark alleyway or behind a door. Come back out a certain amount of time later. Meanwhile, our bystanders are watching out for suspicious behaviour – anyone who might be paying close attention. We're all hooked in on radio with earpieces and phones, and we've got a set schedule for all of this to go down. If someone misses their cue for any reason, the bystanders are well-placed to intervene and check that all is well."

"Makes sense. And for us?" Will asks. "You want us to take a role?"

"Not exactly," Alex says. "You two are getting a bit… known. At any rate, he is."

"Hey," I protest.

"Well, you are. I mean, really, Julius. The SCD9 team know your face better than I do."

I roll my eyes at his reference to what was once called the vice squad. "I don't hang around with sex workers."

"No, but you are so prolific in the Soho scene that there was some speculation you might be one yourself," Alex shot back. "Not to mention that you've probably been drinking in every nightclub in London."

I'm about to retort to that as well when Will cuts me off.

"Where do you want us?"

Alex taps one of the red markers. "Here. You'd better sit inside your car. Good thing it's a rental, so no one recognises it as being yours. We've got two groups gathered close by, as this is a popular area for sex workers. The two hotels at either end of the road. You'll be able to see them both if you sit in this car park, here, with your lights off."

"Got it," Will says, tapping the address into his phone's map for good measure. "We'll head there immediately. Let us know when it's time to stand down."

"It's going to be a long one," Alex warns, before turning away to bundle up his map and head to his own position.

It's a chilly night. Even in the car, with the engine off, I have to pull my jacket tighter around me. Will looks like he's about to freeze to death, so I periodically turn the heating on for a short while to keep him going.

He is poring over notes that Alex left us while I keep watch, lifting his head now and then to report an interesting fact or finding. "It looks like everyone was taken between the evening, around nine p.m., through to two in the morning, according to this. Everyone that we actually know about, obviously."

I grunt. "That's what's so hard about this one. Not knowing what we don't know. There could be others who don't fit the pattern at all."

"That might be the case in every single one we investigate," Will points out mildly. "We just don't know until we know."

"You're annoying when you're right."

We sit in silence for a short while longer, until Will finishes reading the notes and puts the paper up on the dashboard, out of the way. "Nothing much more of use. We're going on the barest possible connections here."

"Well, let's hope it works anyway."

I have a lot of things running through my mind, trying to distract me. I think about what Will admitted to me yesterday morning, and what it means for us. Then there's the aching crawl in my skin, the heat trickling down my spine until I'm happy for the cool air when I loosen my jacket. The twitch in my fingers, that know they are usually holding a shot glass right about now.

"How long have you known?" I ask, breaking the silence.

Will starts and looks away from the undercover officers at the end of the road to meet my gaze. "That I'm...?"

"It's okay to say it out loud now that I know." The smirk I give him is intended as a gesture of affection and reassurance, not mockery.

"It takes a bit of getting used to. I think.... A while. I don't know. There was a guy, back in uni. Before that, I don't suppose I really thought about it much. I was too focused on exams, being the model son, getting a good career. Trying to decide what I even wanted to do with my life."

"I get that," I say, and shrug. "I mean, I was a raving horndog when I was a teenager, but apart from that, I get it. It took me a long time to figure out I wanted to be a detective."

"Me, too. If I even really ever did. I think I just liked the idea of solving puzzles." Will takes a sharp breath. "If I had any idea how bloody and brutal it can really get, I'm not sure I would have gone into training at all."

"I'm glad you did. We wouldn't have met, otherwise." I shift in my seat. "I wish you could have felt comfortable enough to tell me back then."

Will snorts. "Why, so I could have been your first conquest in the Met? We might not have ended up friends if that had happened."

Ouch.

"No," I say, quietly. "I think we would have been friends, no matter what. I liked you for who you are. I never saw you as a potential easy fuck."

"Thanks," Will says flatly, looking out of the window, craning his neck as far away from me as he can.

"I didn't mean it like that," I sigh. This doesn't feel like it's going well. "You're a good-looking guy. As weird as it seems to say that to my best friend and roommate. You're kinda hot, Will baby."

The back of his neck flushes red. "You're right," he mutters. "That is weird."

Is it getting hotter in here, or is it just me? I don't know what I was expecting him to say. That kiss we shared keeps lingering on my mind, even more so now I know that he's gay – and therefore, technically, available.

So, what was that all about?

Maybe I'm putting too much stock in something that wasn't really anything. Maybe it was just a heated moment – me getting carried away, him not resisting for that brief bit of time because, in a way, it was natural for him, too. I guess he sees me as nothing more than a friend. He's made that fairly clear.

"Do you want something to eat?" I ask, stretching and looking up and down the road. "There's a late-night shop still open over there. Mini supermarket. I can get us crisps, sandwiches, drinks. They might even have a coffee machine."

Will shrugs. "I guess I can eat something small," he says. "Coffee would be good, though."

I nod, and duck out of the car, letting the cold air slap me in the face as I emerge. That quiets the fire raging through my blood for the moment, anyway.

In the shop, I grab snacks at random and without prejudice. Anything we don't eat now can easily be taken back to the flat for later. I pick up two takeaway coffees from the machine which is, thankfully, in working order, and then head for the till.

Passing through the alcohol aisle.

And if I happen to swipe a mini bottle as I walk by, and if it happens to fall into my basket as I reach the checkout, and if I happen to down it in one and throw the empty away before I go back to Will – well, then at least it was only a mini.

We spend a long night, huddled in our seats, watching the characters in our fictional cast come and go. Every hour they rotate, moving further down the road, swapping positions. Nothing happens, not to any of them.

With the edge taken off my withdrawal, I am shivering just as much as Will. This is the only thing that makes me resist the urge to take off my jacket and offer it to him. The thought of him wearing my clothes, covered in my scent, marked out as mine – I have to force myself to look out of the window and think of something else, to calm my racing heartbeat and rushing blood.

And when we get the call to stand down past three in the morning, with absolutely no hint of any progress – and we realise that means we have to do the same thing again tomorrow night – I almost want to hit the steering wheel in irritation. If I can't get a grip on myself and these inappropriate feelings, I'm not going to make it through the week – especially without the chance to head into one of my usual bars and find some hot young thing to work off my frustrations with.

TWENTY-THREE – WILL

I was already thinking that we should split up, so it was something of a relief when Webster sent us a text detailing his wife's latest working schedule.

"Looks like I'm on stakeout duty tonight," I said, then amended myself. "I mean, a different stakeout. Ann Webster is staying late, so I probably won't make it to you before you get started. It's probably not a good idea to follow one watching session with another. I'll just fall asleep."

"I guess us taking it in shifts is a better idea, if we're going to be covering both cases," Ram agreed easily. "We don't want to get too exhausted. Alex needs us sharp, even if Pete Webster doesn't particularly."

"That's a deal, then. I'll take this one with Webster, and you can go next time. What about the car?"

"I'll take my bike," Ram said, then paused. "Hey, you know what's funny? Two gay guys spending all of their time watching a married woman for signs of promiscuity."

I cocked my head at him. "That's not really very funny."

Ram laughed, short and sharp, then shrugged. "It used to be. Here was I, thinking that out of the two of us, you were at least interested in women. Then it turns out neither of us is."

I squinted in his direction. "Still not funny."

Ram sighed, throwing me the keys. "Never mind. Sometimes

you swing and you miss, right? Here."

"I'm amazed to hear you admit that you ever miss."

Ram gave me a hard look for a moment, but it was gone just as quickly as it had appeared. "It can happen from time to time."

Whatever that odd look meant, I didn't have time to think about it. I grabbed a jacket and headed out to the car, getting behind the wheel to trace the now-familiar route to Ann's workplace.

Parked outside in the alleyway, I couldn't help but feel restless. There was nothing happening. Not here, and not in the Bonnie and Clyde case. This wasn't how we did things. We got to the bottom of cases, solved them, caught the bad guys. Sitting around and waiting for luck didn't feel right.

Maybe it was time to do something different – take action. If I went inside, I might catch them in the act. For all we knew, they were at it like rabbits in there, while we sat around waiting outside and assumed Ann's innocence when she emerged.

I knew I shouldn't make the decision on my own. I needed a second opinion. We were equal partners in Serial Investigations London, after all.

I grabbed my phone out of my pocket and called Ram, waiting patiently as the dial tone sounded over and over. Just like usual. Why did he never answer his phone?

I gave up and put it down, trying to focus. All I had to do was focus, watch out for Ann coming out. That was all I had to do.

Drumming my fingers on the steering wheel, I tried to convince myself, repeating it like a mantra. *Just watch for Ann. That's all you have to do.*

And even so, I was restless. Bored out of my mind. Too many other things to think about – things that I did not want to confront. It had been a heavy few days. I didn't have enough bandwidth left to sit here and dwell on the difficult things, the questions that were still in my mind about Ram and my parents and whether or not there would ever be a real 'us' where Ram was concerned. Or how I felt about the fact that he was making it painfully, obviously clear that there never would be.

Nothing was happening here. I needed action. A smirk briefly flitted across my face as I realised that I was acting more like Ram – the impulsive and rash one, not the cold logician I tried to be. I opened the car door and got out, barely pausing to button up my jacket before I walked across the road with determination in my stride.

There was little to no security at Ann's office building: an unlocked door leading into a small reception area, with no receptionist behind the desk at this time of the day. I checked out the signs on the wall, which told me nothing since I didn't know what I was looking for, and swiped a parcel which was sitting abandoned on the desk. At least if anyone challenged me, I could pretend I was a courier looking for someone to hand it to.

I pushed through a pair of swing doors into a hallway, painted a dull green and reminiscent of some poor decorating choices in the 1970s. It probably had not been updated since then. To the left, all the way along the corridor, doors sat patiently in their frames, all of them locked. They bore stencilled names in an old-fashioned font – 'copy room', 'accounting', 'records', and so on. Further on, the corridor roamed around a corner, curving into the next part of the building.

None of the doors bore windows, meaning I could not see what was on the other side. It was going to require checking every single room, one by one, if I wanted to track down Ann Webster. That, with hardly a secure excuse for being there, and the very real potential of being chucked out of the building entirely if I came across anything else. Not to mention the highly suspect fact of the DSLR hanging around my neck, quite at odds with my impression of a courier, which could take some explaining.

What could possibly go wrong?

I sucked in a deep breath, and reached for the door handle of the copy room, issuing off a quick and fervent wish to whatever deity, seamstress of fate, force of life and power, or alien overlord might be listening.

24 – RAM

I am sitting on my motorbike, leaning back against the seat, pretending to examine my helmet. Then I glance up and around again, trying to take in any potential changes since my last look. Still nothing.

It's a tedious night. Without Will's company, left without anyone to talk to, I quickly run out of things to occupy myself with. Just looking isn't enough. With looking, your mind ends up wandering as much as it likes. And sometimes, you don't like the places that it wanders to.

Like the feel of Will's soft mouth against my own, the heat of his breath licking over my lips, that brief and sweet moment when he almost relaxed into my touch. Before he was freaking out and gone, slamming his bedroom door behind him, to pretend that nothing had ever happened.

I let out a groan, my breath dissipating into the cold air in a cloud of white that is swiftly gone. I'm glad no one can hear me. I'm torn between wanting to punch something, and giving up on all of this and getting on an app to find someone for a quick fuck.

Except I'm not sure that I want to do that at all, anymore. Because everything's different now, isn't it? As much as I can pretend that it's not when he's around, it is. Thinking about Will – it's no longer just a silly fantasy. Not now I know that he's gay.

Now I know that the very shape of my body wouldn't automatically be a turn-off for him, that one stolen kiss has taken on a completely new meaning. I guess not for him. He was just exploring things – giving in to his newfound acceptance of himself.

But for me, it has become something else. A possibility. An opening.

Which I can never take, because of course then I would lose my best friend.

I get off my bike, resting the helmet on the seat, and crouch beside it, examining the body and tyres. I need to busy myself. I keep a cleaning cloth inside the seat compartment, and I grab it now, starting to polish all the silver and chrome detailing to make it shine.

Down here, I also have a good opportunity to look up and watch the groups of people outside the bars a few doors down. Their conversations carry to me in snippets on the wind, bursts of louder laughter and screams or squeals of playful drunk flirting. How I wish I could be drinking with them. The double whiskey I had to strengthen myself before settling into position has all but dissipated, the warmth no longer fuelling me from the inside.

Nothing is really happening. This is the tedium of the stakeout, the watchfulness that is never really fully explored on television. They show you a montage, detectives almost falling asleep in their cars, getting doughnuts and coffees to keep themselves going. That cannot convey the way it really feels. The way time moves at a snail's pace for hours, and an hour can pass in the blink of an eye, both at once. How every night is different, really, no matter how many times you do it.

Tonight, I just really want all of this to be over.

The small hand-held radio I had stashed in my pocket crackles, announcing an incoming message. I dig it out and hold it closer to my head, behind the body of the bike where no one will see it, just in time to hear someone hurriedly repeating the name of a fellow officer.

"PC Nettle, come in. Unit Sixteen - PC Nettle. Please confirm your whereabouts. PC Nettle!"

There is a long pause on the line, silence filled without even a crackle, everyone in the whole chain holding their breath to wait for a response.

"All officers, alert. I have lost line of sight on PC Nettle. She is unresponsive. Last seen with a potential suspect, near the entrance to the Tube at Old Street."

"What the hell is going on?" Alex's voice, cutting through the crackle, harsh and demanding.

"Sir, I believe she went with them into the station. A bus passed by and obscured my view. Radio signal may not be strong enough down there."

"All units in vicinity of Old Street station, converge on the entrances and exits. One officer to be left at each. The rest of you, into the station and tracking down PC Emma Nettles. Do it now!"

I bite my lip, realising that I have been holding my breath. This is happening, and happening now. I watch the officers at the end of the road and in front of the bar, how they look to each other in concern, their tiny earpieces picking up the conversation. One by one they casually begin to move away from their positions, gravitating towards one another.

"Unit Seventeen, in position at exit three."

"Unit Eighteen, in position at exit two."

"Unit Fifteen, in position at exit four."

"Unit Fourteen, in position at exit one."

I close my eyes momentarily, visualising the station with its long, sloping, double-sided exits and the eerie blue and green passageways inside. The bustling shops and stalls – flower sellers, coffee shops, even small clothing brands. How many of them would still be open at this time of night? Any of them? And how busy would the station be?

It only services the Northern line, so easy enough to figure out where someone is going to or coming from. But it's a major hub, especially with the Shoreditch nightlife kicking off just a short distance away. Drunk people, the homeless, people heading home from late nights at the office or heading into night shifts. The officers searching could waste precious time checking amongst the faces there, looking for their colleague.

The line crackles again, another voice coming over. "Unit Seventeen, station appears clear. No sign of PC Nettles or the suspect."

I swear under my breath, no doubt at the same time as many others also listening in.

"Unit Seventeen, request that you approach station staff for playback of surveillance camera footage. Find out where she's gone." Alex sounds desperate, his words clipped and his tone harsh, everything said in a rush of one breath.

Moments tick down. I get up, put the rag away, and lift my helmet. If something is going down, I feel like I'm in the wrong place. I should be there, doing something. But it isn't as though I can call Alex and ask for permission. This is his case, and all of the pressure is on him now. He needs the line clear for communication.

"All units," his voice comes through again, a little higher pitched, a little more strained. "Converge on rendezvous point, exit four at Old Street Station, for new briefing. Repeat, all units converge now on Old Street Station fourth exit!"

I shove the helmet on my head, barely pausing to do it up, and kick my bike into action. I will arrive quicker than almost all of them – beating those on foot easily. The quicker I get there, the better.

I almost collide with a taxi driver, who leans out of his window to shout curses at me in an unfamiliar language as I speed off. There are only a few streets between here and there, and though one of them might be the busy Great Eastern Street – a favourite for late-night revellers – I push the accelerator forward hard, easily breaking the speed limit as I approach the rendezvous point.

I spot him easily, Alex already standing to the side of the exit, a handful of officers gathered around him from the nearest positions. I park up on the pavement – another fairly illegal move – and head over, taking off my helmet as I go.

"Nothing?" Alex is saying as I approach, tugging a hand back through his hair, clenching a fist in it. His face is pale, sheened with sweat. "How can that be possible?"

"I'm not sure, sir," the young officer beside him says. "It's possible she got into a vehicle or walked around the corner, rather than going into the station. I can't see anything on the cameras."

"Fuck!" Alex explodes, stabbing at the screen of a tablet in his left hand. "Search parties, immediately. You two, head down that street there. You two, to the left. We don't know how fast they were moving, so you'd better run. Keep your eyes peeled. Go!"

"What can I do?" I ask. "I have the bike. I can move faster than those on foot."

Alex looks up, his eyes searching, analysing every inch of the roads around us. "Down there," he says eventually, pointing towards one of the four spokes from the Old Street roundabout. "Turn onto East Road. Look out for anything suspicious. If you can, check the back seats of the other vehicles on the road."

I nod, not wanting to wait for further instructions. I have heard enough. If there is a policewoman stuffed in the back of a car, being driven to a dungeon against her will, it should be obvious to see. I will know her if I see her.

I think briefly of calling Will and letting him know what is going on, but there's no time. I jump back onto my bike and kick it into gear, nearly causing another collision as I pull out into traffic.

I slam my hands against the handlebars angrily, relishing the sting of pain that blossoms over my palms even through my thick leather gloves. Fuck this. And fuck Bonnie and Clyde.

I reach inside my jacket and find the miniature bottle, swiped from a minibar last time I was in a hotel and refilled as a makeshift flask. It sits where it always sits, right inside my leathers, ready for emergencies.

I grab my phone out of my pocket and dial, trying not to give in to frustration as the engaged tone sounds out four times before I finally get it to ring.

"Anything?" Alex bites off.

"Nothing," I say, trying to force my thick tongue and throat to work together. "I went as far as seemed sensible and then carried on for another five minutes. Nothing suspicious of any kind."

"Come back to Old Street." Alex's sharp words are punctuated by the call ending, the buzz of the city in the background of the call silenced and replaced by my own surroundings.

They still haven't found her. I know it by the fear in his voice. I'm not the only one whose search was unsuccessful. I unscrew the lid of my bottle and put it to my lips, waiting for that welcome burn that will soothe all of this down.

"No." I say it out loud, to myself and the universe. *No.* This is not the time. I need to focus – I have to stay alert. I have to help save this woman's life, stop her from being imprisoned in that place that Ray Riley and Simon Shystone never came out of. I can't do that drunk.

I fling the bottle against the floor, watching it smash against the pavement next to the residential parking space I have squeezed my bike into. There's some lovely shards of broken glass for people to cut themselves on. Always making these impulsive gestures, never doing the right thing. Fuck.

I don't have time to hate myself for it right now. There's only one thing I have to do, and that is to find PC Emma Nettles and bring her back.

Before I do as Alex says, I dial another number. We need all hands on deck for this. And that means Will, too.

TWENTY-FIVE – WILL

I hovered with my hand over the handle to the first door in the newer wing, hesitating. What was that?

I heard it again a moment later, and I knew I hadn't imagined it. It was only a low sound, quiet enough – the kind of thing you might miss, unless you were deliberately creeping around a corridor as quietly as possible.

It wasn't coming from the door I had been about to open. I stepped forward, heading towards the middle of the corridor. There it was again – a low, throaty moan, quickly stifled and caught in someone's teeth.

I forgot about the parcel entirely, dropping it on a windowsill and leaving it there. The prop wasn't important anymore – not if I was hearing what I thought I was hearing.

I focused in on the unmarked door, approaching it with as much caution as I could, wincing at even the light taps of my feet on the polished floor as I moved closer. At least I had opted for boots, instead of trainers that would have left the squeaky noise of rubber moving against a smooth surface.

There could be no mistaking. The sound was coming from behind this door, and as it came again, I couldn't have any doubt as to what I was hearing. A woman, caught in the throes of passion, unable to control the moans issuing through her throat. I stopped just in reach of it, lifted my DSLR to my face, and kept one finger on the trigger.

Then, with the other hand, I reached out and carefully, slowly, pushed the handle down.

I was in luck. It was in good shape, perhaps oiled recently – there was no hint of sound as I smoothly and slowly opened the door, just a tiny crack. I was ready, tense and primed, to hurriedly push it the rest of the way and act if there was anything that would give me away, but nothing did. I hesitated, their moans and even the sound of their bodies coming together much clearer now. They hadn't noticed a thing.

I pushed the door open and let it go, swinging smoothly out as I focused through the lens and returned my other hand to stabilise the body. As soon as I could see them, I snapped off a succession of fast shots, rapid machine-gun fire as quick as the camera could manage it.

And what a collection of shots they would be.

Because there was Ann Webster, spread-eagled across a desk and totally naked, looking up at me with a comical expression of utter shock as her lover paused, still deep inside her.

Whoever he was, he was certainly not Pete Webster.

"Who the hell are you?" The man found his voice, features furrowing into an angry scowl as Ann screamed and covered her chest with her hands.

I simply grinned, and read the tension in the room. This was not the kind of man who was going to let me go and carry on with his activities. Not when I had just taken plenty of pictures of him and his lady friend *in flagrante delicto*. No, if he was quick enough to catch me, there was going to be a beating – not to mention the destruction of my very expensive camera equipment.

I didn't give him the chance to recover. I turned on my heel and ran, knowing I had enough shots already to prove to our client that his fears were not unfounded.

There was a kind of exhilaration in the chase, which was only compounded when I hit the main entrance doors full force and found that they opened inwards – a fact which I might have remembered from my ingress if I hadn't been too full of adrenaline to think properly. I fumbled for the handle as I heard his pounding footsteps moving down the corridor behind me, reminiscent of nothing so much as Bigfoot, King Kong, or the T-Rex hunting down his victims.

I burst out into the cold chill of the evening air, the sun already down and gone, and rushed over to my car. By the time he had exited the building – still totally naked, clutching a pair of trousers against his groin to protect his decency – I was starting up the car. I offered him a cheery wave as I drove by.

Watching him receding in the mirror, I couldn't help but laugh.

But the laughter died as the adrenaline wore off, my heart pumping slower as I caught my breath. I pulled over on the side of the road, wheels propped up on a pavement, fighting a wave of dizziness. I hadn't had dinner or brought anything with me to eat, and the burst of exertion had taken its toll.

Resting as I was, I checked the screen on the back of my DSLR, flicking through the pictures I had taken. A few were blurry, a result of my shaking hands and the movement of my subjects. But the quality didn't matter. It was plain to see that this was Ann Webster in every particular – right down to a birthmark on the back of her right thigh which left no room for denial.

I'd caught her red-handed. The job was done. So, why did I feel so rotten?

I would have to be extremely cautious with these photographs – better to show them to Pete Webster instead of sending him the files, in case I was somehow accused of distributing pornographic images without consent. If anything, it was miserable that I had anything to show him at all. I had been hopeful that he was wrong – that Ann Webster loved her husband and just happened to work hard.

Or even didn't love him, and chose to come to work to avoid him – what difference did it make? But this, this was not the result I had wanted.

How could people treat each other like this? Saying 'I do', swearing a vow of fidelity and loyalty, promising to love one another forever – and then turning around and sleeping with another person? As much as I realised that I was not quite like other people with my approach to sex – that maybe it mattered more to me because it was not something that I considered lightly – I couldn't understand the emotional betrayal.

And I couldn't stand the fact that this played right into Ram's worldview, his stubborn insistence that sex was meaningless and monogamy was for idiots. He would probably love this, crow about it for weeks afterwards.

Even so, I couldn't just delete the photos and pretend that I hadn't seen a thing. Pete Webster deserved to know the truth, however difficult that truth may have been to swallow. I set the camera aside with a heavy heart, and turned on the ignition, thinking about going home and getting some sleep.

My phone buzzed on the seat beside me, lighting up with Ram's name. Typical of him to give me a call back long after I needed his opinion on what to do.

"I've got news," I said, dispensing with the usual line of greeting.

"So have I," Ram replied, and the grim set of his tone had me sitting up straighter in my seat.

26 - RAM

I am running on nothing more than fumes. Looking at Will, I can see he feels the same.

"We need to be smarter about this," I say, tapping the maps and plans that have been dredged up out of some basement for us. "We have to think. Rushing through it isn't going to help if we miss a vital clue."

"Just hard not to rush, when someone's life hangs in the balance," Will sighs, rubbing a hand over his bloodshot eyes. "Every single minute, all I can think about is whether they've already started torturing her."

"You're not the only one," I reassure him. Glancing around the incident room, I take in the drawn and haggard faces of the skeleton crew left behind to look for clues and signs that can't be found at the site of PC Emma Nettle's disappearance. Everyone looks worried, upset, tired. We've all been up since last night, trying to track her down.

The ground searches have so far found nothing. Numerous residents have been given rude awakenings during the early hours of the morning, as police asked for permission to enter and search their homes, especially those that have underground floors. With the proliferation of flats London is known for, this is no small task.

The area around Old Street is largely commercial, which has also led to a long night and morning for those manning the phones, trying to call and locate those with the keys to let officers in. Garages and warehouses, offices and storage units. However likely any of them may seem, each has to be checked and searched. A huge blown-up map of the local area has been posted up over the top of a slew of other notes that once occupied a noticeboard, and someone is dutifully colouring in each building, one-by-one, as they are searched and cleared.

Meanwhile, Will and I pore over blueprints and building permission documents, trying to find and identify anything within a reasonable distance which has underground construction of any kind.

"This is pointless," Will groans, reaching for his coffee cup and throwing it back into his mouth, only to find it already empty. "Would you really be inclined to get planning permission for your underground sex murder dungeon?"

"No," I admit. I don't want to say it, but I'm afraid he is right. The building that we are looking for might not even be on these plans. But at least we're trying something. "Let's just get through this stack. At the very least, we can keep directing Alex's teams to places that we know have underground structures. If those don't pan out, we move onto the next plan."

"Which is?"

I have no answer for him. I push my hair – which is getting long enough to continually fall into my eyes, probably a sign that I need a haircut – towards the back of my head, and knuckle down at cross-referencing maps with blueprints.

The morning ticks on, coffee cup by coffee cup. I am sweating again, my body crying out for the nectar I smashed on the ground last night. I want and don't want it, in equal measure. I feel like I am being split in two, and the headache is only part of that. I fumble for another ibuprofen, only to find Will's fingers laid firmly on top of mine.

"You've had the maximum recommended dose already," he says, not looking up from his blueprints.

"It's only a painkiller," I scoff. "It won't kill me to have a couple extra."

Will does look up now, meeting my eyes with a grave and steady expression. "It might, with the abuse you've given your body lately. And it's a little insensitive to use that kind of language right now, don't you think?"

I have no argument against that. I sigh and look back at the last few plans on the table, collating the data as quickly as I can so that we can move on.

Once the information is given over to one of the officers Alex chose to stay behind, so that he can relay locations to the teams on the ground and get them into position, I get another bitter, burnt coffee from the office machine and sit down heavily.

"What do we do now?"

"We should do it our way. Alex called us in to be consultants, right? There's a reason for that. We've got some way of doing things which is different from everyone else. We should be doing that, not just following orders."

I nod. "That makes sense. But what *is* our way of doing things?"

"Logic and thought," Will says, biting his lip. The movement distracts me so completely that I have to shake my head, sending another throbbing round of pain rattling around every side of my skull. I close my eyes and clutch at my head for a moment, waiting until it diminishes enough for me to breathe again.

When I open my eyes, Will is looking at me with pity, which I instantly dislike.

"What can we ascertain about location?" I ask, trying to change a subject which neither of us has even broached.

"Most killers target an area which is within a reasonable distance from their home. We know this already. There's a certain distance which is close enough for convenience, and far enough that they feel safer."

"But we're in London, which means that target area could cover quite some distance."

"True." Will thinks, tipping his head to the side. "Let's think about this. If you don't have planning permission to build an underground chamber, you have to do it without arousing suspicion. But that isn't easy in the middle of a city."

"Construction at the same time as something else," I say, thinking of the hammering in my head. "Noise to hide noise. Equipment, materials, all the rest of it. Hidden in plain sight. Maybe an extension, conservatory, remodel, something like that."

"Now you're thinking," Will snaps his fingers. "Alright, and the construction must have been done before Katie was taken, which was two years ago. Take into account the fact that she thinks she wasn't the first one, and we can look at maybe a one-year range before her abduction."

I drag my chair over to the side, to the computer terminal we have been assigned. Although it is, at least, marginally better than the old huge-framed boxes of the nineties, it isn't much better. I guess that's what happens when you have budget cuts all over the shop.

"I'll search planning permission records. We're looking for a residential street, you think, right?"

Will ponders it, humming lightly. "It is possible that it would be on a commercial property, though perhaps not probable. Include those as well. Who knows, maybe a commercial property was having construction done and they took advantage of it next door."

"Good thinking. And we have to look at a certain radius."

"It's tough to be sure, at this point. I wouldn't rule much out. But let's start with maybe one mile from Shoreditch High Street."

I nod, inputting the data. This feels topsy-turvy. Will is usually the nerd in the computer chair.

A whole page of results loads – and I watch as it continues to populate, the results spilling over into multiple pages that we will have to click through.

"This… may need narrowing down," I say, turning the screen so that Will can see it.

He whistles low, then nods. "Okay. First thing I think we should do is mark down every street that had construction within our search area and timeframe. Then we can cross-reference that list against the homes of known sexual predators, people with violent convictions, and so on. We might at least get a few hits that seem more promising than others."

The scale of the task ahead of us makes my head spin and my stomach protest. I clutch my skull again, holding back a groan.

"We'll get through it," Will says. He lays a hand lightly on my shoulder, warm and reassuring. "Just think about her. PC Nettle. Whatever you might be going through, she has it so much worse."

"I'm not sure it's a competition," I mutter, but his words hit home. More so, his touch on my shoulder, reminding me that I have someone at my back no matter what.

Having Will around is probably something that I've been taking for granted for a long time. That ugly jealousy that rose up in me when he struck up a friendship with Harry felt a lot similar to the fear of losing him. Which I still might do, if I don't at least try to clean my act up a little.

Not very rock and roll, but then again, I've been trying not to become my father for my whole life. Coming off the alcohol sure would be a step in the opposite direction to his story.

I'm not sure I can do it, but there is one thing I know. It's that I need Will. Whatever new configuration we will find ourselves in after everything has settled down – even if I need to adjust to him bringing his boyfriends round to the flat, and putting in headphones so I can't hear them fucking all night long – I can't let him get away.

Even if it makes me sound like a little kid, he's my best friend, and I need him.

We work on the profiles for hours, using the police records to find last known addresses for a large number of offenders who fit the bill. It turns out there are criminals all around us, whether we know it or not. Any innocuous-seeming neighbour could be a wife-beater, a rapist who got away with it because there wasn't enough proof, or prone to fistfights outside bars.

When it's done, we still have hundreds of potential addresses. The morning has drained away like sand into the bottom of an hourglass, and PC Nettle is still out there.

We take the list to Alex's second-in-command, DS Fox. The man is at least ten years older, with brown hair peppered with grey and a seemingly permanent crease across his brow, the result of a long career spent reading files and interrogating miscreants.

"What's this?" he demands, casting an eye over our map with little interest. I get the feeling that he resents being stuck at HQ, in charge of the paperwork and computer searches, while Alex gets right in the middle of the action.

"Addresses that may be worth checking out," I start. "We've got a theory about construction work that -"

"I don't want theories," DS Fox says, moving away from me. His accent is flat and hard, a true Londoner. "I want facts. I'm not wasting manpower on a wild goose chase."

"If we're right, these could be real leads," Will says.

"If," DS Fox repeats, turning back to us with a sneer. "Could be. One of my colleagues has put her life on the line. I'm interested in finding her, not chasing fairy tales. DI Heath might have put his faith in you, but as far as I'm concerned, you're amateurs with too much time on your hands and too much of Daddy's money in the bank. I take leads from real coppers – not Sherlock bloody Holmes."

He stalks away and immediately begins talking to a PC who has just entered the room, leaving us staring at his back.

"Okay," I say, more to myself than anything else.

"Looks like we're going to have to work through these ourselves," Will murmurs, taking the map from my hands and leading me back to our desk.

"How are we supposed to do that? Go out there and walk the whole fucking route? We can't even knock on doors. We're not police officers."

"We don't need to walk around in the real world to find anything," Will says solemnly, giving me an absolutely straight face. "We have the internet."

TWENTY-SEVEN - WILL

I wasn't fully confident that we were going to be able to narrow it down enough. Records could only go so far, and there was always the risk that our profile – still stuck to the wall in front of our cramped, shared desk – was meaningless. That we had mistaken one thing for another, made an assumption in the wrong place.

But we had to do something, and working towards a smaller list of potential addresses was better than staring at the wall and twiddling our thumbs.

Lunch was a pile of greasy crumbs left on a plate, and we had drunk so much coffee that the machine was close to overheating by the time we had made any real progress.

It was painstaking work, going through each potential suspect manually. The first thing was to ascertain what kind of offence they had been arrested for. Sexual or violent crimes went right to the top of the list. The closer to what we were looking for, the better.

But that wasn't much to go on, particularly when the vast majority of flags seemed to be for assault, ABH, or something of a similar nature. There had to be more. We had to pick out more from the records, something that would tell us about the person who could commit these kinds of crimes. Hitting someone when drunk at a football match was a very far cry from locking someone up and torturing them for months.

A few times, I almost thought I had it. A man who was arrested for domestic violence, near a house that had had to be rebuilt after a fire. He had grown up with divorced parents and had a son living with an ex-girlfriend. But he was single and living alone. No Bonnie to his Clyde.

They were all like that: almost perfect until they weren't. I kept a list of these near-misses, a lot smaller than the list we had started with. At least it was something. We had to allow for a little variation from our profile, after all.

Diana Hunter swung into the office a little after three in the afternoon, carrying an overnight bag and a large takeaway coffee from a national chain. I looked at it longingly, thinking how much better it must have tasted than the swill that was keeping us awake.

"What are you working on?" she asked, immediately intrigued by our maps and slews of paper records.

"We're using the profile," I explained. "Trying to narrow it down to a location where PC Nettle could have been taken. I'll explain it all if you want. Where have you been?"

"Visiting my parents for what should have been my weekend off," she said. "I was in Glasgow when I got the call. Let's just say it's been a long drive."

"You don't have a Scottish accent," I remarked.

She shrugged. "Neither do they. So, talk me through this process."

Diana was sharp. Once I had explained everything, she jumped in with gusto, helping us search through the records we had and eliminate unlikely suspects. Even though she must have been behind the wheel for a long time, she was at least looking at the records with fresh eyes. Just when we were flagging, she gave us renewed vigour, the energy to keep going.

I blinked, and reread the file I had been staring at. It was getting hard to look at the computer, my eyes feeling gritty and sore from the lack of sleep. Was I really seeing it correctly?

This man had no criminal convictions, although that did not mean that his record was clean. He had been arrested a couple of times in the past, brought in on allegations of sexual assault. Nothing had been proven. One of the cases had made it as far as court before being dismissed for lack of evidence.

So far, so normal.

But then I dug a little deeper, checking his family name. Soon I had a hit on his mother, a woman who had been brought in many times on charges of being a sex worker, as well as other offences. She was a drug addict and alcoholic, judging by the tale that her arrest record told. Not a good upbringing for a young boy – especially the kind of young boy that might, later on in life, use his experiences as an excuse for bad behaviour.

I dug a little deeper. My suspect was married to a woman a few years younger than him, though she had no criminal record. But it didn't matter. She didn't need to have one in order to be Bonnie.

A little deeper still, and I found the man listed on his birth certificate as the father. A different surname to my suspect and his mother. Most likely an absentee father, then.

A search of the father's name found a LinkedIn profile, an impressive resume of a man with grey hair and a stern expression in the photograph at the top of the page. He had risen to an executive position in his company, and his profile also contained images of his wife and adult children. Neither of whom, I noted immediately, were my suspect.

"I… I think I have a hit," I said, calling Ram and Diana's attention.

They read over my shoulder, eagerly watching as I moved the mouse with a shaking hand, showing them what I had found. "Look. Sexual assault arrest record. An absentee father who has a successful career and a stable home life with his other children. Mother was a sex worker, which ties into this want to humiliate them. And he has a wife."

"Construction?" Ram asked.

"A pub two doors down, the summer before Katie was taken – July 2015. They added a new extension and remodelled their beer garden with paved areas. Plenty of concrete, steel, bricks. They would have dug out some earth for the foundations, which could have been a good cover for Clyde to excavate under his building."

"Their residence?" Diana peered over my shoulder at the map, pulling it towards her, ready to search.

I rattled off the address for her, putting my finger down on the exact location. "Two floors, one bedroom. It's been in his family for a long time. Looks like his grandparents bought it long enough ago to be able to afford it, and his mother took it over when they died. He followed suit."

"They have land behind the house?"

I studied the aerial view I had opened on an internet search. "A small garden, it looks like. Nothing more than a strip of grass."

"Room to move in tools, hold materials for the short term," Diana said, snatching the map off the table with her eye firmly on the place I had indicated. "I'm calling Alex."

"Not if I call him first," Ram grunted, digging his phone out of his pocket.

28 – RAM

"This is probably a very bad idea," Will says, hesitating in the passenger seat.

"Will, baby," I say, leaning over and fixing him with a serious look. "Don't you trust me?"

"Absolutely not," Will retorts, screwing his face up. "Last time we were in a situation like this, I ended up nearly getting killed."

"After I warned you not to go in. And who was there to rescue you before things went too far?"

Will massages his neck as if he can still feel the bruises that lingered for long weeks after our brush with the Highgate Strangler. "I'm just saying. Maybe we shouldn't be taking any chances."

I know he is right. Of course he is – he's Will. But that doesn't change the fact that I feel like I need to do something.

"What if this is her? Alex is still planning strategies, marshalling forces. We're here now. We could make a difference."

Will sighs. "He told us not to go in alone. To wait for him. The fact that he has to make plans should probably tell us something about how sensible it is to rush in without one."

"I have a plan," I insist. "We just take a look. Quiet as church mice. We'll go around the back, through that gate on the side."

"It's probably locked."

"Then we'll climb it." I pause for effect. "Quietly."

Will shakes his head at me. "I don't know why I'm arguing. We both know we're going in eventually. The only difference is whether now or in two minutes."

"What's the safe route to a couple of sinners like us?" I say, only half joking. "Come on. We'll be covered by the darkness."

I get out of the car, closing the door gently to avoid making a clatter, and wait for Will to join me. We stand looking at the house, on the other side of the road and four doors down. Just enough distance away to not draw too much attention where we were parked.

"Ready?" I whisper.

Will nods at me, illuminated only by the single working streetlight at the other end of the road, his features thrown into sharp shapes by the harsh shadows.

We cross the street stealthily, watching the ground for broken glass and our surroundings for loose objects that could make any kind of noise. We stay on the pavement, away from the motion sensor zones of neighbour porchlights, making our way closer to the address.

Will passes in front of me on the way to the front of the house, then rushes forward on almost silent feet to the wooden door set next to the property, clearly leading back to the garden. My breath catches in my throat as I run after him, hoping that they aren't looking by chance out of a window at that moment.

Despite my confident words in the car, fear is crawling up my throat, a slow choking thing that wants to strangle my breathing. I am not afraid of getting hurt or putting myself in harm's way. I never have been.

I'm afraid of Will getting hurt – of seeing him lying on the floor like that time when I thought he might have been dead.

"You wait here," I whisper directly into Will's ear, my words so quiet I can barely hear them myself. "I'll go over. If they come out, stall them."

His cold ear brushes my lips as I pull away, not giving him time to disagree. A shudder runs over me, but I ignore it to grasp hold of the top of the wooden door and pull myself slowly up. No sense in risking a creaking hinge or a heavy, rattling lock somewhere out of sight.

It takes all of the hard-won strength I have been building up in my regular gym sessions to pull myself over the other side and drop down, quietly, only making a little noise as my feet hit the floor. I'm quite relieved to see that they don't have a dog – a possibility I only even began to consider just as I was touching down.

They don't have much at all, actually. A few scattered items that have clearly been discarded, a deflated football that probably came over the fence from one of their neighbours, and their bins, arranged in a neat row.

I hold my breath as I pass by the windows, looking over to see with relief that the curtains are closed in all of them. It's a dark night. Almost all of the windows in the neighbourhood have their curtains closed. Still, there is no accounting for luck.

I lift the heavy lid of the black, general-use rubbish bin, doing it as carefully and slowly as I can. I imagine it slamming down against the body of the bin, bouncing back, making enough of a racket to pull anyone's attention. I ease it carefully into place, then peer inside.

It stinks. No surprises there. I hold back a gag as I try to make out the contents by the light of the moon alone, a task which proves impossible on this cloudy night.

I take out my phone, wincing internally at how potentially stupid this is. Especially if they really are the Bonnie and Clyde we're looking for. I lower it as far down into the bin as I can to at least shield some of the light from reaching the house, and switch on my screen.

Reflecting the light, mangled and smashed to pieces, are the parts of what is still recognisably a police radio. The kind that

PCs carry as standard kit.

I swallow hard, my heartrate amping up to even faster than it was already. I don't need to see a nametag to know whose radio that is.

We've found PC Emma Nettle.

And that means we've found Bonnie and Clyde.

My heart is in my mouth, and I can barely hear anything above my own breathing, loud and ragged even though I try to quieten it down. I switch my phone onto the camera and take a quick shot, then lower the lid as carefully as my shaking hands are able.

It drops back into place with barely a noise, but I still freeze, my gaze darting across all of the windows of the house to ensure the curtains are still closed.

I swallow, trying to ease the dryness in my throat, before crossing the garden back to the gate. I step in my own footprints, desperate not to stray from the known safe path and step on anything that might make a noise.

And now I have a new problem: getting back over the fence.

It wasn't as terrifying when I didn't know for sure that a pair of serial killers live in this house, and would show no qualms about abducting me into their torture den – and probably Will, too, if he stuck around to try and stop them. Now I have to deal with the fact that if they hear me climbing over, we could be in real trouble.

Not just us, either – what if they realise they are being watched and decide to kill PC Nettle in response?

"Will," I whisper, barely above a breath, hoping he can hear me through the wood.

"Yeah?"

I close my eyes briefly in relief. "I found her radio in the bin, smashed up. This is it."

"Are you coming back over?"

"It's too risky. Will, call Alex. Tell him we've found Bonnie and Clyde. Ask him for backup."

I hear a gentle sigh from the other side of the gate. "I don't want to leave you here."

"I'll stay right here, out of sight. Go back to the car. Please, Will. We can't take any chances. If I fall and make a loud noise, it's all over."

I wait, listening to the sound of Will breathing. Gentle and quiet, but quicker than it should be. He's scared. I have to admit, I am too.

But when I hear his footsteps moving away, I can breathe a little easier. I want Will out of danger, safe, somewhere these people can't hurt him.

As soon as he's far enough away that I can't hear his footsteps anymore, I make my move.

TWENTY-NINE – WILL

I walked back to our car on light but frantic footsteps, paranoid now that any one of them could give Ram away. I couldn't see any sign of movement up and down the road. We were in a residential area, and it was the middle of the night; sleepy and quiet.

The loudest sound of all was my heart pumping in my ears, surging faster and faster. Propelled by the fear of Ram stuck in the lion's den. Trapped with merciless killers who could maim and scar even if they spared his life.

I was careful not to slam the car door as I jumped back inside, firing up my phone and calling Alex as quickly as I could.

It went to his answerphone. I swore, cancelled the call, and tried again.

"- DI Alex Heath." He sounded rushed, broken off, like he was in the middle of another conversation.

"Alex, it's Will," I scrambled, my words coming out on top of one another, so fast I wasn't sure he could understand me. "We've found them. Confirmed location of PC Emma Nettle. We need backup, now."

Alex barked off an order to someone else, asking for their ETA. "We're ten minutes away from you. Stay out of sight and away from the house. We'll be there in a moment."

I glanced out of the car window back towards the property, and my heart dropped like an anvil into my shoes. "That might be difficult," I said.

It was Alex's turn to swear. "What has he done?"

"He's talking to them," I said, squinting through the darkness. "To Clyde, I think. At their front door."

"For the love of – *why?*"

I didn't have an answer for him.

"I have to go," I said. "Back him up. Just get here fast."

I put the phone down and leapt back out of the car, barely registering Alex's last words about *jeopardising operation* and something else I didn't catch. Whatever he said, he was undoubtedly right. This was one of the stupidest things Ram had ever done.

Even if it did give me a small moment of opportunity to realise how Ram must have felt when I barged in on the Highgate Strangler to try and stop him from killing his last victim. Terrified. Powerless. And out of anyone, he should have known that going in alone was a stupid decision.

"Here he is," Ram was saying, as I got close enough to hear. "Like I said, we just can't get the car going. Normally I would just call for recovery, but I guess my insurance ran out a week earlier than I thought."

I understood the part he was playing right away, even if it didn't sit well with me. This was 2018. There were much easier solutions to this problem than knocking on someone's door. Clyde was just going to ask us why we didn't –

"Why don't you just call a garage?" Clyde asked.

And there it was.

"We're not local," Ram shrugged apologetically. "Can't get any signal on my damn phone, either. You wouldn't happen to have the details of a garage around here, would you?"

Clyde grunted, his face creased into a frown heavy with bushy eyebrows. He was halfway to closing the door. "Can't help you."

"Look, please," Ram said, urgently, taking a half-step forward. "We're going to be stuck out here all night, and it's cold. Most garages are closed by this time. I just need a number I can call to get some help, but without signal, I can't search for a twenty-four-hour place. I just want to get back home."

I wanted him to stop, to let them go. Let them think we were just a nuisance, nothing more. I couldn't stand this. Looking Clyde in the eye, talking to him. Knowing what was going on under his feet.

"What's going on?" A female voice this time, from deeper inside the house. A woman emerged into our view in the slim line of the corridor we could make out behind Clyde, a brunette woman with a pinched face and greasy, straggled hair.

"Car breakdown," he said, glancing us over again. "Couple of blokes asking us if we can look up a garage for them."

"At this time of night?" Her laugh was shrill and unpleasant, clearly at our expense. "You'll be lucky."

"That's what I told them." Clyde leaned over his shoulder to look at her, his thick beard brushing across the top of his polo shirt. It was stretched across his frame – broad and barrel-chested, maybe that of a man who had once been much fitter. They were older than I had imagined, both of them. Perhaps in their forties or even later. They didn't fit the profile of most killers, who would start in their teens or twenties. If Katie Wood really had been one of their first victims.

I could feel prickles all over my skin, goosebumps that were reinforcing the message my brain was sending to all of my limbs. *Run. Get away. Go now.* I laid a hand on Ram's arm, thinking that I could lead him away before they stopped us.

"Why'd you knock on our door, anyway?" Clyde asked, eyeing me in particular.

"We saw the light on through the curtains," Ram lied. It sounded weak to me, an excuse that no one would buy. "Figured someone was home, so it was a good place to start."

Clyde leaned out of his doorway, forcing me to take an involuntary step back. "But you're parked down in front of number sixty-two, and their lights are on."

Ram flashed him an easy smile. "Maybe your house just seemed more inviting."

"He's a nervous one, isn't he?" Bonnie peered over Clyde's shoulder, her black eyes fixed on me, glittering darkly. I thought I saw something in her hand and flinched. It was just a phone.

"I-I'm just… I didn't think it was a good idea to bother anyone," I stammered out, my mouth dry and empty. My palms were slick with sweat, my body primed to run.

Behind them, their entrance hall stretched, dark and covered in murky wallpaper, spiderwebs hanging from the doorframe. I swallowed, remembering another corridor that I had rushed down with abandon, maybe not caring that I could have died. I remembered a vice tightening around my throat.

"Maybe it wasn't," Clyde said, glancing up and down the street as he took another step forward. He was fully outside of his own property now, joining us on the cold step, his presence physically towering over both of us. "You boys are alone, are you?"

"Yeah," Ram said, and I could hear the uncertainty in his own voice now, the nerves, the fear.

I started to rationalise in my own head. There was a way out of this. We just had to be patient. It was easy enough to get away clean and free. Wrap up the conversation. Apologise. Retreat to the car. Wait for Alex to arrive. Stay out of the way and let the police do their job. Simple, simple, simple.

"You didn't let anybody know you were here? And you weren't told to come here by anyone?" Clyde took another step closer. I stepped back and lost my footing, scrambling down from the broad step onto the pavement. "Say, the police?"

Ram laughed, false and strained, a higher pitch than normal. "Why would we be with the police? Are you guys drug dealers or something?"

Clyde growled, a sound that came from low in his throat, seeming to rumble through my whole body. "What kind of game is this?" he demanded.

"We made a mistake," I said, tugging at the sleeve of Ram's leather jacket. "We'll just go back to our car, and -"

"And call for backup?" Clyde stepped forward again, Bonnie almost out of the house behind him. "You think we're stupid? You're cops."

The irony of the fact that we were not at all cops forced a nervous laugh from my lips, a sound I barely recognised as my own.

"Like Will said, we'll just -"

"No, you won't." Like a whip, Clyde's hand shot out, grasping Ram's upper arm in a vice and pulling him a half-step forward. "You're going to come inside and enjoy some of our hospitality."

I was frozen, stuck in limbo. Every single part of me that wanted to run was now anchored in place, tied down with fear. Not for myself, but for Ram. I could have run then, made it back to the car. Clyde was unarmed. He couldn't have stopped me.

But I couldn't just leave Ram to figure his own way out.

Ram was pulling back, struggling to get the other man off his arm. Holding him at the perfect length, Clyde pulled back and punched him hard on the jaw, with a sharp clack that I felt all the way down my spine. Ram went limp for only a moment, and that was enough for Clyde to yank him forward, sending him crashing into the corridor. I started forward without thinking, and before I even knew what was happening I was following him, Clyde offering me a simple shove that left me tangling my legs with Ram's and hitting the ground.

I couldn't breathe. We were trapped – again. Two of them and two of us. It was all over. There was no way we were getting out of here safely – and as Clyde slammed his front door shut, leaving us in the relative gloom of the unlit corridor, I knew that there was no way we were getting out alive.

30 - RAM

I look up, catching my bearings, ignoring the pain in my arm where I hit the floor and the pain in my knee where Will tripped over me. For the moment, that is more than inconsequential. If I don't get back to my feet, we will be in deeper trouble – and more pain is sure to follow.

I manage to get up and stare them both down, my eyes shooting in both directions. Clyde in front of me, Bonnie behind. Will is curled up on the floor, gasping for breath, maybe winded or hurt. He can't defend himself. My head whips from side to side, not knowing where to go first.

"Let's get them downstairs," Clyde snarls, aiming a swift kick at Will's legs.

"Hey!" I try to pull his attention, going for him, only succeeding in throwing my body against the wall. He side-steps me with a lightness on his feet that seems impossible, a bounce that speaks of training. A boxer, maybe, past his prime but still capable.

I have to take my attention off Bonnie to face down Clyde, and when he looks over my shoulder with a wicked sneer, I know it was a mistake. I glance back and see Bonnie re-emerging from a doorway she must have ducked through, the light from that room reflecting from something metallic in her hand.

A knife.

I have no time to think, only to react. No time to consider the repercussions or the fallout. My instinct is to back away, although that only brings me closer to Clyde – but when Bonnie lunges towards Will, who is just starting to try to get up from the floor, I don't hesitate. I won't let him get hurt.

I would die to save him.

The knife catches skin as I push him out of the way, ripping a path along my forearm. It pulls deep, a strange sensation, the feeling of my own flesh parting. The moment is gone and I crowd Will against the wall, behind the protection of my body, still watching both sides. Bonnie and Clyde could take us down at any moment. They have a weapon, they know the layout of the house, they have us surrounded. They have raw brute strength over us.

Hope begins to drain away, like the blood I feel easing out and down over my fingers, when I realise that they are playing with us.

They could have us down there, tied up, ready for their torture. It would only be a few moments of struggle, and we would lose.

The only reason we're still upstairs is because they're enjoying this. If I wasn't convinced of it already, the evidence is in the looks on their faces: wild, savage joy, wicked fascination underscored by lust and anticipation.

We're fucked.

Adrenaline still surges through me, but as they approach, getting closer and closer on either side, I can also feel the throb of pain. The cut on my arm is bad, and my fast-beating heart is only pumping blood out of me quicker. At my back, I feel Will, his hands on my shoulder blades, his breath quick and hot on my neck.

I don't know what to do or how to get out of here. Bonnie flashes the knife towards me, chuckling low and throaty when I flinch away, and I know that it doesn't matter what I do. They have us. Like foxes trapped in a snare, watching the hounds approach with spittle drooling from their mouths.

"Armed police!"

The shout goes up outside, and all of our attention switches, going to the door. It is solid wood, no window to the other side. No way of knowing what's out there.

The momentary break in their advance turns into a stall, and then Bonnie is retreating back down the hall.

"Come out with your hands above your head!"

I look at Clyde, and Clyde looks at me. And I know he won't be getting out of here without a fight. I can't get us caught in this. We have to get out, and now.

I take a chance, grab hold of Will's hand with my good one as Clyde lurches past us after his wife. I reach the handle of the front door and tug it open, remembering at the last minute to throw my hands up above my head. Drops of warm blood splatter down onto my head from my fingertips, their direction abruptly reversed.

We run out, stepping out of the way as Alex barks the order to enter. Swarms of police in body armour and helmets rush past us, yelling commands and warnings, dispersing through doors after the now-vanished Bonnie and Clyde.

The hurricane passes by us, and someone is trying to force us down to our knees before Alex is there, pulling us out of the way. Someone presses something against my arm – cloth – stinging and burning – and I look for Will and panic when I can't find him.

"W-" I don't even manage the first syllable before I see him again, to my left instead of my right, being led in a stumbling run by another officer, both of us moved back across the opposite side of the road. Alex hands me over to someone else, and I dimly recognise Diana Hunter standing well back behind a cordon of cars, here to witness the final takedown.

"Sit," someone orders, and I rest on the edge of an open car boot, the vehicle dipping slightly with my weight. My arm is raised up above the level of my chest and bent as the person beside me carefully peels back the fabric to examine my wound. I feel a hot surge of blood against my skin before it is placed back and they are shouting for paramedics, calling someone over from the other side of the cordon.

I have lost Will. I scan around for him again, ignoring the man in green overalls opening a first aid bag at my feet. There – over by Diana – she is reaching over to take him by the shoulder, pulling him back into safety, asking him questions. I catch a glimpse of his white face as he looks back in my direction, then is pulled away.

There is shouting inside the house, drawing the attention of everyone around us except for the paramedic pressing a cool patch against my arm, sticking it down, making me lose my breath with the pressure on the wound. More shouts, and then a single gunshot, loud enough to seem to reverberate through the neighbourhood.

I am back in San Francisco and I close my eyes on rooftops, then open them again on a house in London.

I am aware of something rushing towards me, and I turn in fear to see it is Will, broken through the cordon again and hurrying to my side. He touches my shoulder and I know everything that he wants to say at that moment but can't in front of witnesses. How every time he hears a shot he, too, will be back there on a rooftop. How he is grateful that we can share this together, instead of suffering through it alone.

Alex emerges from the house first, talking into a radio at a rapid pace, moving out to give orders to others around us. A police van sits ready with its doors open, and the paramedic rushes away from me towards the entranceway. He stops, hesitating to one side with his female partner, as a group of policemen march out. Bonnie is carried between them, shouting and screaming blue murder, her face contorted and twisted.

They take her into the van, and the paramedics are gone. After a few minutes of tense wait comes a stretcher, a white sheet wrapped around a figure. Clyde. There is fresh, red blood on his face. He goes into the waiting ambulance, and another replaces it, a new pair of paramedics rushing in.

I can barely breathe. A glance around at those assembled and waiting to play their part in this shows that neither can anyone else. We all need to know.

And then another stretcher emerges, carrying on it the prone body of PC Emma Nettles. I recognise her from the circulated images we were given, even in profile. Her skin is ashen and her face tear-stained, black marks of makeup tracing their way to her chin. But she is moving – her bare arm reaching up towards a colleague before she too disappears into an ambulance and is gone.

"Thank you," Will whispers at my elbow, and I turn to look at him.

There are tears in his eyes, which he can't drag away from my arm. I look down and realise the state I am in: the bandage the only thing clean on me, everything else splattered with crimson drops already darkening. My fingers are smeared with it, my arm a story of rivers and rivulets, both up and down.

"I didn't want them to hurt you," I say, finding my voice.

Will clutches my shoulder, then withdraws his hand, as if afraid of pressing too hard. "You got hurt instead."

"And I'd do it again." I know it is true as I say it. The words ring like a bell, pure reality. I would. I'd jump in front of a knife or a bullet or a fist or anything for Will's sake. The way he looks at me right now, the warmth and gratitude in his face, the receding fear, is the only reward I would ever ask.

"Get him to the hospital as well," Alex barks as he draws near us, pointing at me and addressing the nearest officer. His face is pale, too, and he blanches more when he takes in for the first time the blood that I am spattered with. "Julius, I swear to god. I told you not to charge in on your own."

"You told Will," I point out, managing to pull out a grin. "I never received any such warning."

"If you're not dead by the end of the day, I'm going to kill you when we debrief," he says, shaking his head. "Will, I'll call you later. Keep him in your sights. No more reckless behaviour."

"Don't worry," Will says, and I can't help the shiver of giddiness that runs through me. "I'm not taking my eyes off him ever again."

THIRTY-ONE - WILL

In the end, Alex didn't catch up with us until the next day. We'd been told to stay at home, to rest – particularly for Ram's sake. Seven stitches hid now under the white bandage wrapped around his forearm, seven stabbing needles of guilt. He was hurt because of me.

It was almost lunchtime when Alex rang the intercom to be let into our apartment building. I hurried to get it. Despite Ram's protests that it was only his arm that was hurt, I had been insisting on him sitting on the sofa while I did everything he needed. He complained every time, but with a sly smile that crept onto his mouth every time I began to turn away.

"Ready for your debrief?" Alex asked. "I have to apologise. I ended up crashing last night at the hospital, waiting to hear about PC Nettle's condition. By the time the doctors woke me, I had my sarge pressuring me to go home and rest. Then this morning, there was the press conference to deal with."

We hadn't watched in on the news. I'd been too worried about Ram, and he had slept until only an hour or so ago. I had been unable to, getting up to check that he was alright every fifteen minutes, snatching only a brief shut-eye here and there.

"How is she?" Ram asked, as I sunk down on the sofa beside him and gestured for Alex to take our sole armchair.

"Recovering," Alex said, hesitant as he searched for the right word. "I won't call her fine. She suffered a number of wounds in the time she was missing, most of which were inflicted with a pair of pliers. The doctors say the skin will grow back. Her tooth won't."

"Fuck." Ram shook his head in regret.

"They had her tied naked to the chair, just like Katie and Jodie described. The one upside to all of this is that we don't have to push hard for evidence. It's obvious to everyone that Bonnie and Clyde are responsible for the abductions of all three women. Real names, by the way: Mark Davidson and Kim Martin. Not that anyone is likely to remember them, when they've already given the press the best possible nicknames to use."

We all paused, quiet hanging heavy. Outside, a bird was singing somewhere, perhaps in one of the decorative trees planted in the pavement. PC Nettle was not going to recover from this kind of ordeal very quickly. It had happened under our watch, all three of us, even if we weren't exactly responsible. That was a sobering thing to deal with.

"We found a few things that fill in gaps," Alex continued, picking at a loose thread on the trousers of his cheap suit. "There was a video of Adelaide Walters walking through London, taken from some distance away and without her knowledge. We now believe that they used this footage to blackmail Ray Riley into appearing in Kent and telling police he was fine, to avoid suspicion. As soon as they stopped looking into him, he was returned to the dungeon. Still not clear on how Jude Hargreaves fits in, but it at least explains Riley's behaviour."

"Was our profile close?" I asked. "We thought that Clyde would be punishing father figures who played away or abandoned their children, and Bonnie had some kind of resentment towards sex workers. Maybe she, or her mother, was one, as well as his. We got the details on Clyde – that's how we tracked him down. But Bonnie came up clean."

"Same for us." Alex spread his hands in a gesture of powerlessness. "Who knows? Maybe she doesn't have a tragic backstory. Maybe some people just have it in them to do evil things."

"Everyone has it in them," Ram said, quietly. "It's just that most of us have a conscience holding us back from acting on it. I would hazard a guess that she was drawn into it by Clyde's predilection for violence, and found she enjoyed the schadenfreude a little too much."

"How's your arm?" Alex asked.

"Fine." Ram turned it to examine the bandage as if he hadn't yet seen it. "It throbs a bit. Might be a pretty impressive scar."

Alex rolled his eyes. "Is everything with you just about whether or not it's more likely to get you laid?"

"No," Ram said, quieter still, and the atmosphere in the room had changed without my noticing it. It felt cold now, and there was something going on with Ram, something that made him studiously avoid both of our eyes to seek out the floor.

Alex's phone rang in his pocket. "Sorry," he muttered. "I'm waiting for updates. We've got a team in with Bonnie now, still interrogating."

I lifted a hand in absolution. When his terse and brisk conversation resulted in him making a gesture of apology and heading for the door, I was hardly surprised. Alex Heath was going to be a busy man for a long while over this. I didn't expect we'd get another look-in for weeks, at the very least.

Which was fine, because we were also expecting a visit from our other client: Pete Webster. Breaking another man's heart wasn't high on my priorities list for the day, but he had to know what we had found. That was what he was paying us for, after all.

We waited with a kind of nervous energy for Webster to arrive. At least this was a little better than our last client case – we wouldn't have to tell him that his wife was dead. Just that she slept with other men.

I cast my gaze sideways, looking at Ram from under my lashes. He was preoccupied with his phone and didn't notice me watching him. His blond hair had fallen into his eyes a little, disturbed from his usual messy-neat style where he pushed it back over the top of his head. I had to smile a little to myself;

even here, sitting casually at home after an exceptionally long couple of days and after being discharged from hospital twice, he looked like a rock star. His dark shirt was open just one button too many to be formal, and two leather bracelets were stacked haphazardly over the tattoo on his wrist.

"When did you get that tattoo?" I asked. I realised I had never heard the story. It had just always been a part of him.

"Oh, that?" He lifted the ink closer to his face, chuckling at some memory that I was not privy to. "When I was about fifteen. Drove my mum crazy."

"Pretty good choice, for a fifteen-year-old. It's aged well."

Ram moved one of the bracelets with a finger, studying the black silhouette of a crow permanently etched on his skin. "Guess it has, at that. Twelve years of fading. Probably helps that my tattooist was the same guy who's done half my dad's. I had a good reference for what it would look like over time."

I looked at that tattoo, and something wild and out of control inside of me wanted to know what it would be like to lick and kiss that ink. To find out if it tasted the same as the rest of his skin.

He knew I was gay now, and he still hadn't made a move. The kiss must have been a mistake.

But what if the real mistake I was making was not making it clear that I wanted him – all of him? That I wanted to do it again and see what happened?

"Hey, R-Ram," I said, scratching that itchy spot on the back of my head, shifting towards him in my seat. "We should -"

And whatever we should have done was lost, because that was the precise moment that our buzzer sounded again.

I got up to let Webster in, rushing to the intercom. When I turned back, Ram was watching me with a strange expression on his face. Almost like he wanted to laugh.

"What?"

"We should, what?" he asked. His lips quirked up at the sides before flattening out. There was something in his eyes I hadn't seen before. At least, not directed at me.

I coughed and turned to open the door just as Pete Webster arrived in our hall.

"Come in, Mr Webster, and take a seat," I said, deliberately avoiding meeting Ram's eyes as I took my place on the sofa. "We have some updates for you."

Webster settled down on the armchair that Alex had occupied not half an hour before, and regarded us with a grave expression. He looked as though he was about to find out in what manner his death sentence was going to be carried out. I understood at that moment that he already knew what we were going to tell him. He had always known. We were just bringing him the proof.

"We've prepared a file for you," Ram said, placing his fingers on the green folder sitting on our coffee table to spin it towards Webster. "I want you to prepare yourself. We followed your wife and took some photographs. They will not be pleasant to look at."

"I'm ready," Webster grunted, and somehow I could not doubt it. There was a sheen of sweat on his brow, whether from the climb up our stairs or the knowledge of what he was about to see, I could not tell.

"If you're sure." Ram lifted his hand away, leaving it free for Webster to take the file.

He lifted it to his lap and opened it, and pulled out the colour photographs I had printed for him. Frame by frame, they told the whole story of his wife's deceit. Ann Webster with her legs wrapped around her co-worker's back, her body wide open for him. The two of them turning in shock. Their mouths opening into screams and shouts. Him turning, no regard for her decency as he revealed her to my lens.

There could be no doubting or disputing what I had captured. Ann Webster was caught in the act, in full detail. Pete's eyes watered as he looked at them, his hands shaking, his mouth moving in a dance of words that he did not speak.

"Thank you for these," he said, at last, putting the photographs back in the file and pushing it towards us.

"Those copies are for you," I told him, keeping my voice low and respectful. "We have the digital files as a back-up. You can take them home."

"I don't want to." Webster wiped the back of his arm across his eyes, sniffed a little, and then did something that surprised me entirely. He smiled. "The thing is, it doesn't really make a difference. I suppose I already knew. I just didn't want to admit it."

"Don't you want them for the divorce proceedings? Proof of infidelity?" I asked.

"There won't be a divorce. Thing is, gents – if you can believe it – I love my wife. I love her a lot. I thought this would change things, but… looking at them now… Even if she is having an affair, I'd still rather be with her than without her."

He laughed, getting to his feet with a kind of joyous energy that seemed incredulous to me.

"What will you do?" Ram asked.

"Go home, and tell my wife how much she means to me," Webster said, laughing and wiping at his eyes again. "I've been an idiot. Sorry to have wasted your time. I've got to go and work on my marriage."

He left us, a gale of strange laughter following him down the stairs, leaving me watching him go from the doorway.

"Well, that was unexpected," Ram said.

I closed the door and shoved my hands in my pockets. "I don't get it."

"You don't?"

"How could he possibly forgive her? She betrayed him."

"He loves her."

I looked up at the way Ram's voice seemed to catch on those words, and his expression made my heart stop for a moment. He was wistful, dreamy even. Not the sarcastic, practical, sometimes caustic man I was used to.

"Doesn't that make it worse?" I asked. "He loves her so much, and she threw it away anyway."

"When you love someone," Ram began, then hesitated. I stole back towards him, sinking soundlessly onto the sofa beside him as he gathered his thoughts to continue. "When you love someone, they can do a lot of things. Hurt you, break your heart, do things that other people would condemn them for. But that doesn't necessarily mean you stop loving them."

"But cheating?"

"Emotional cheatings is..." Ram broke off and corrected himself. "From what I imagine, emotional cheating is different from physical. If she still loves him heart and soul, and has no emotional feelings for the other man but just needed sex, it's easier to forgive."

I shook my head wordlessly.

"You don't agree?"

"I don't know." I rubbed my eyes with the heel of my hand. "I've never been in a relationship. I guess it seems like it should be black and white, like all cheating is bad. But maybe it's not."

"Not even in school?"

I glanced his way. I couldn't help the amused smile slipping onto my face. "Trust you to zoom in on that, and ignore the rest of it."

"Alright. I don't think it's black and white at all. I think it's all grey. Theory is all well and good, but maybe you can't really say how you'll feel about something happening until it does. And there are different circumstances around every time it happens.

Now," Ram shifted towards me, leaning his head on his hand against the back of the sofa, lifting his knee up onto the seat. "You didn't even go out with anyone in school, without it really meaning anything? Not even a girl, just to try it?"

"I was a good student," I said, shrugging. I let the rest of it slide. I couldn't really argue with him, never having gone through the experience yet. "I wanted to make my parents proud. I didn't need distractions."

I shifted my body in a mirror of his, then froze when I realised what we were doing. This – this was exactly how we had been sitting when it happened. *The kiss.* When Ram didn't pull away, I swallowed hard and tried to relax. This was me over-reacting, right? Like always? He probably hadn't even noticed the similarities.

"What about now?" Ram asked. "Now that you're coming out, you could meet someone. A boyfriend, maybe."

That prickling feeling was moving up and down my spine again, that voice in my head urging me to be reckless. To throw caution to the wind and lean in for the kiss. It hadn't forced us apart last time.

But I couldn't be sure that Ram would react the same. *Different circumstances every time.* I licked my lower lip, feeling how my mouth was suddenly dry.

"I'm surprised you're not encouraging me to get on Grndr and find myself a one-night stand, like you do."

Ram shook his head. His blue eyes bored into mine, like diamond drills, seeking the truth. "You're not like me," he said. "You're... you're a virgin, aren't you?"

I felt my cheeks heating up with a deep flush. There was no point in denying it, not when he had asked me outright like that. I couldn't hide behind lies when it was written all over my face. "... Yes."

"Then you shouldn't be on one of those apps, looking for a quick hookup." Ram reached out, to where my arm lay across my knee, and adjusted the folded hem of my jumper sleeve. "You should stay away from guys who just want a quick fuck and then won't ever call you again. Guys like me."

"What's wrong with guys like you?" I asked. My voice hitched in my throat, getting low and husky. I'd never heard myself sound like that before. My heart was speeding up, going a mile a minute. I craved that touch. I fought the urge to mess up my sleeve so that he would reach out and fix it again.

"I hurt people."

"You saved me," I said, moving my hand to trace the white edge of the bandage covering his forearm.

"But you're – you," Ram said, his eyes following my fingertips.

"And we're talking about me."

I didn't know where I'd found the courage to say something like that. It was out before I could reason with myself not to say it. In the pause before he spoke again, I knew he had understood the subtext that was playing out between us. I might not have been experienced in these things, but I knew Ram. I knew how to read him.

"Your first time should be special. Considered. Not just with anyone."

I caught the way his eyes flicked over my lips, the bob of his Adam's apple as he swallowed. The air between us felt heavy and hot, like a humid night. I felt a rush of something magic in my blood, something that made me brave and made my voice speak.

"You're right. I want my – my first time to be with my best friend. Someone I can trust…" My eyes fell down on his forearm again. "Never to allow me to get hurt."

He swallowed again, then raised his chin, his eyes connecting with mine like a lightning bolt. He reached out, a motion both practised and hesitant at the same time, and stroked his fingers along the line of my jaw.

I shuddered, and Ram's fingers drew back as if I had stung him. I grabbed hold of them before he could take them fully away, held them there against my skin, told him as much as I could with my eyes that I wanted them. Wanted him.

Encouraged, he leaned in closer, pausing only a moment before his lips swooped across mine. The first brush was fleeting, too fleeting, a touch that left only the ghost of sensation behind. I stretched my neck out, found and claimed his mouth again, pressing against him with a desperation that came from deep down inside of me. A need that had been unanswered for too long, caged and restrained, and now would have its day.

When his mouth moved in response, giving way to his tongue, opening before me, it was like a slice of heaven. I had wanted this for so long – dreamed of it, when I even dared that much. Now it was happening, finally happening. My world narrowed to a single point, the juncture of his mouth with mine, the way we danced and swayed together.

He broke off, and for a terrible moment, I thought he had changed his mind. One look into his eyes, dark with something unnameable, told me I was wrong.

Ram reached down under the cushion of the seat he was sitting on and drew out a silver flask. I should have been mad with him for hiding it, but I found that I couldn't be, not just then. There were things happening that were beyond the control of logic, of the normal range of emotions. The only setting I had left was lust, raking over me like fire, making me want to beg for his lips on mine.

"Here," he breathed, unscrewing the lid and pressing it into my hand. "Courage. You might need it."

I tilted my head back, taking a shot. The rough burn of whiskey trailed down my throat, making me want to cough. I grimaced, then caught Ram watching me with a look of such strange fascination on his face. His eyes were trained on my mouth, his hand coming up to my jaw to hold me in place as he took my bottom lip between his own. The sucking sensation was maddening, and then his tongue swept and swirled inside my mouth, tasting every drop of whiskey left behind.

I panted for breath as we parted, my hands clutching for him, almost forgetting and dropping the flask. He took it from me and downed his own shot, though what he needed courage for I did not know. He set it down on the coffee table with a clatter and pushed me, his hands flat against my chest. My back hit the sofa cushions, my own hands darting to the front of his shirt to pull him down over me, closer, to where I could reach his mouth again.

His hair fell down as he stretched out over me, the ends of the strands tickling my forehead. "Are you sure about this?" he breathed, so close to me that it could have been his thoughts I was hearing.

"Yes," I said, because it was simple, and that was all that was needed, and I didn't want even a moment's more delay that would keep his skin from touching mine.

32 – RAM

Ringing… ringing…

My phone is ringing.

Shit!

I force my eyes open and fumble on the table beside my bed until my fingers connect with a familiar device. I hit the mute button on the side, then turn it over to blink at the screen through eyes crusted and fuzzy with sleep. *Alex Heath*. Must be about the case.

There's a small noise by my ear and I turn my head to see Will settling deeper into the pillow beside me, still just barely asleep. The weight of his arm over my chest is comforting rather than restrictive, the heat of his body warming rather than oppressive. Despite the sunken cheeks and the fear that hit me, more than once, last night that I might snap his frail body in half like a twig, he is beautiful in rest.

For the first time in a long time, I don't have the urge to creep out of bed, get dressed, and go before he can assume this was more than a one-time thing. I just want to lay here and soak in the feeling. Bask in it. More – I want to hold him here, safe against the world, until he is better. I want him healed and whole again.

Which is why it's a shame that my reach for the phone has stirred him, and he slowly opens his eyes, blinking at me.

The spell is broken. And if Alex is calling at this time on a Saturday morning, supposedly his weekend off, it must be important.

So much for a moment of morning bliss.

"Yeah?" I say, lifting the phone to my ear. My voice croaks, a part of me that is still waking up.

"Julius, I've got some bad news."

I sit up straight, knocking Will's arm aside. He grunts a surprised complaint before sitting up himself, gathering the covers over his naked body, concealing. I can only spare half my attention to that. From Alex's tone – beaten, weary, sleepless – I know it must be seriously bad.

"What is it?"

"Post mortem for Simon Shystone. We were waiting for the results when PC Nettle was abducted, and – well. Now we know."

Beside me, Will is starting to slide out of the bed, making for a pile of clothes on the floor. I grasp hold of his arm, momentarily startled by how it fits entirely within the ring of my hand, and pull him back. "What's wrong?" I ask Alex, switching the phone to my other ear so that Will can lean his head against mine and hear it too.

"The pathology, it's… it's all wrong." Alex sounds like a man at the end of his tether. Like he might just break down at the end of the next sentence, if he even makes it that far. "He isn't one of Bonnie and Clyde's victims. At first, we thought it was just down to a bit of variation in their games. But the report came back, and most of his injuries were inflicted after death, not before. After we brought her in, Bonnie folded like a house of cards, told us everything. She admitted to a number of abductions we hadn't even heard about, both male and female victims. She insisted Ray Riley was the only one who ever died, and that it was a mistake. She'd never even heard of Simon Shystone."

"So, what does this mean?"

"It means we've still got one more killer on the loose," Alex says, uncharacteristically rough and terse. "And we can't even ask Jude fucking Hargreaves, the only person who might have some clues, because some idiot let him kill himself in a cell that was supposed to be watched."

There's a loud crashing noise in the background of the call, followed by a curse. Alex kicking or hitting something, or knocking something to the ground.

I lean my head to catch Will's eye. He looks as shaken as I feel. "The investigation isn't over."

"Not by a long shot."

Alex ends the call without so much as a farewell, but I can't say I blame him. The man has a heavy weight on his shoulders. For us, it's just about saving lives. For him, it's a mortgage.

"We'd better get up," Will says. "There's work to do."

"I need a shower first. You?" I say. I lean towards him with the intention of pulling him into another kiss, a flirtation that I envisage ending with the two of us panting in hot, steamy air. But I almost fall onto his side of the bed as he moves away, standing with his clothes clutched in front of him.

"I probably should," he says, distantly. Then he shuffles sideways towards the door, looking everywhere but at me.

For a moment he pauses in the doorway, and I think he is about to say something. Instead, he clamps his mouth shut and darts away, and I hear the door to his own room shut a moment later.

I stare at the space where he was, then flop back down onto my pillow, the space we shared only a few minutes ago. So, what was that about? Was last night just about fucking and nothing else? It sure as hell didn't feel like that to me when he was moaning my name into my mouth, or when we finally fell asleep, exhausted and sweaty and still holding one another.

But now he's gone, and I am confused and frustrated again, not knowing where I stand.

Except for the fact that there's a murderer out there somewhere who hasn't been brought to justice, and it's still our job to bring him in.

At least that's something I can work on.

I linger just one moment longer, breathing in the scent of Will's shampoo on my pillow, before forcing myself up and into my bathroom. Maybe tonight, or tomorrow, or next week we can figure this out. Sit down and have a real talk. Maybe I will admit that I think I might be falling, hard and fast, for my best friend.

But today, there's a killer to catch. And that's exactly what we're going to do.

CODA

He drums his fingers on the desk, a frown furrowing his brows. These boys – so stupid. Falling prey to their emotions.

Did they even catch his last hint? If they didn't, the game can't continue. They won't know to look for him. And if they don't know, they will never find him.

This is what he wants, of course; but there is a difference. He wants to win by virtue of being the best player, not because they just stopped playing.

An alert sounds from his monitor, and he wakens into action, opening the email. An attachment sound file, a recording taken from his monitoring software. He presses play and listens with his head cocked, beginning to smile.

"Yeah?"

"Julius, I've got some bad news."

"What is it?"

"Post mortem for Simon Shystone. We were waiting for the results when PC Nettle was abducted, and – well. Now we know."

Aha. The joker in the deck – the ace in their sleeve. DI Heath, coming to their rescue yet again. He wonders idly whether such a man should be eliminated, for the purposes of evening out the sides for the final round.

"The investigation isn't over."

"Not by a long shot."

He smiles, broadly now. It isn't over – not by a long shot. Oh, and they barely even know it yet. They will be on the right track, after all. He opens another program and checks the cameras, sees the open balcony outside the apartment where one of them stands with a bowl balanced in one hand. Julius Rakktersen. Alone. Even on the grainy image, it is easy to work out which of them is this small, faraway figure. William Wallace rarely ventures out onto the balcony, and he would certainly never stand there shirtless.

They are apart again, their emotions controlled. Good. So much the better: something else that he can use against them.

There is a glee welling up inside of him at the thought of this final stage, the last test they must pass before he will allow them the honour of facing him directly. No one has made it this far before; no one has been so clever. Unsolved cases litter the path that falls behind him.

But now, at last, he will know if he has found his match. He eases back into his chair, letting the soft leather seat soothe the lines of his body, and lights a celebratory cigar.

The game, as a certain literary character he once admired would have said, is afoot.

READ MORE

Enjoyed this book? Then sign up for Rhiannon's mailing list at rhiannondaverc.co.uk – and get your hands on a free short story download!

Subscribing also gets you release announcements and newsletter-only exclusives, including snippets from Ram and Will's case files, live event announcements, giveaways, the chance to join launch teams for future books, and more. Sign up now!

"Erm, has someone been going through my archives? Looks like some of my serial killer files are missing…" – William Wallace

Become a VIP

If you love Serial Investigations, why not become a VIP? You'll get special goodies as well as access to books before they are launched to the general public. And you get to be part of the launch team for each book, ensuring that the series gains a wider audience!

To sign up, head to rhiannondaverc.co.uk/vip and enter a few quick details.

AND LAST BUT NOT LEAST...

"Amazon and GoodReads reviews are important for every author, and we really appreciate every single reader that leaves one." – William Wallace

"And those of you who don't can fuck off!" – Julius 'Ram' Rakktersen

"..." – William Wallace

Follow the latest news...

Website - rhiannondaverc.co.uk

Twitter - twitter.com/rhiannondaverc

GoodReads - goodreads.com/author/show/16733877.Rhiannon_D_Averc

Amazon - http://author.to/rhiannon

Printed in Great Britain
by Amazon